A Case for the Cookie Baker

A Case for the Cookie Baker

An Ainsley McGregor Mystery

Candace Havens

TULE
PUBLISHING

A Case for the Cookie Baker

Copyright© 2021 Candace Havens
Tule Publishing First Printing, June 2021

The Tule Publishing, Inc.

ALL RIGHTS RESERVED

First Publication by Tule Publishing 2021

Cover design by Sue Traynor

No part of this book may be used or reproduced in any manner whatsoever without written permission except in the case of brief quotations embodied in critical articles and reviews.

This is a work of fiction. Names, characters, places, and incidents are products of the author's imagination or are used fictitiously. Any resemblance to actual events, locales, organizations, or persons, living or dead, is entirely coincidental.

ISBN: 978-1-954894-35-8

Chapter One

GEORGE CLOONEY COUGHED in the corner, and I swear he shook his head. I couldn't blame him. We'd been in Classroom C, upstairs in my shop, Bless Your Art, for more than an hour.

My fellow crafters and I had been discussing what kind of float we should have for the Sweet River Fourth of July parade. Thanks to the mayor, who decided this was a great way for the chamber of commerce to celebrate local businesses, everyone in town was scrambling to figure out what to do. I'd never built a float before, so I thought it might be helpful to get input from all of my vendors.

I was wrong.

"We could do a jungle theme," Mrs. Whedon, my favorite octogenarian, said. "I can knit some cute little monkeys and Don and Peggy can cut some palm trees out of wood."

Don, who looks like Santa and is usually just as happy, frowned. "I don't see what the jungle has to do with a shop that sells arts and crafts."

"And wine," Mike chimed in. He and my best friend Shannon had a winery at the edge of town.

Mrs. Whedon huffed. "It would at least be more memorable than your suggestion of all of us sitting on hay bales knitting and doing crafts. Besides, I'm old and my bones don't like hay bales."

I had to bite my lip to keep from smiling. I glanced down at my phone. It was edging toward six, and it was girls' night. My friend Jasmine had invited a few of us to come out to her new house to see the work that had been done there.

Carrie, who was sixteen going on forty-five, raised her hand like she was in school. I pointed the cookie I'd been munching on toward her. "What is it?"

She blushed. "I think we can all agree that the biggest celebrity at Bless Your Art is George Clooney. People will come in just to say hi to him. So, what if we did a float of George and then had different things that represent the shop around him."

For the first time in an hour, there was complete silence. Carrie cast her eyes down to the floor. "Or not," she whispered.

I wished I hadn't just stuck the rest of the cookie in my mouth so I could say something.

"I think it's a fantastic idea," Don said.

"You are such a smart young woman," Mrs. Whedon added. "That's the perfect float." If the crankiest person in the room agreed, getting the rest to go along wouldn't be difficult.

I loved Mrs. Whedon—she was family to me. I called her Gran. She'd made herself my honorary grandmother last Christmas.

Everyone nodded, and a big smile spread across Carrie's face. "I thought each of us could maybe come up with ideas that represents our arts and crafts," Carrie said. "I'd say they need to be at least two feet tall and about as wide, so they can be seen from the street. Maybe we could do some sketches and come back next week with our ideas?"

George grunted beside me as if he were giving his approval. All eyes turned toward me.

I swallowed the rest of the cookie and nodded. "If George thinks it's a good idea, so do I. Though, I'm worried it might all go to his head."

George sighed, and cocked his head.

Everyone laughed.

"I like Carrie's thoughts about doing some sketches. It's late and we should get going." Finally, I had to get out of here. I hated missing a second of girls' night.

I'd never had best friends like Shannon, Jasmine and Lizzie. We were almost like sisters, well, ones who got along. Lizzie was the newest member of our little gang. She's so adorable. When she first opened the shop, for some reason Shannon thought her name was Sheila. It wasn't until Jasmine asked why she called her Sheila instead of Lizzie that she realized her mistake. When she asked Lizzie why she didn't say something, she shrugged. "I thought it was a cool nickname or something," she said.

Everyone filed out of the conference room. George stretched and then tooted. That, mixed with the new perfume Gran was trying out, was not doing my stomach any favors. She had a date with the judge tonight, and had dolled up before the meeting.

"Dude, that is so gross but I'm glad you waited until they left. I'm guessing you need a walk before I drop you off at the firehouse?"

He took off for the back door to the shop, and then

grabbed his leash off the hook by the door.

"All right then."

We headed out into the park that followed the river behind my shop. He trotted along happily as if he didn't have a care in the world.

"Come on, dude. I have places to go, and don't you want to hang out with Jake?"

He squatted, but was interrupted by a jogger, who was running really fast.

Growling, he lunged at the figure.

"George. That's mean. Stop it."

He pulled hard on the leash but I yanked him back.

"I mean it. No treats for you if you don't calm down."

At the "T" word, he grumbled but finally sat.

My shoulder hurt from where he'd yanked it so hard.

I couldn't be mad though—he'd been trapped inside most of the day. And was probably hungry and in need of a good run around the yard.

I'd never seen him go after someone like that unless he was tracking a bad guy. He was the kind of dog who usually loved humans a little too hard. Sometimes knocking me over when he leaned in too much.

My phone rang and I glanced down to see who it was.

I punched the button. "I'm on my way, soon," I said.

Shannon, my best friend and favorite coffee shop owner, laughed. She looks like Margot Robbie and is always up for an adventure. "We are all here and were wondering if you had an ETA."

"Tell the gang I'm sorry. Our float discussion went longer than expected."

"I can understand that. It's our busiest season besides Christmas, and the mayor wants to stop everything to make a float. It's nuts."

"So you still have no idea what you're doing either."

She chuckled.

George started to tug me to the right as we neared the shop. "Stop that," I said to my Great Dane. "You already hurt my shoulder."

"What happened?" Shannon asked.

"George was startled by a jogger. He nearly pulled my arm out of the socket."

I tightened his leash, but he pulled me toward the bakery and then whined.

"Lizzie isn't there, silly. No more cookies." Get Baked, was her bakery. She'd only been open for a short time. The name had created a bit of controversy, but she'd held her ground.

It didn't hurt that she made the most delicious cakes, cookies, and pies. Lizzie Hernandez had magic in her because her creations were also addictive. I didn't really blame George. I'd eaten three cookies today. And she always saved a few of the not-so perfect ones for my dog.

"You are not going to believe this house, well, mansion," Shannon said. "It's incredible what she's done already."

Jasmine, who made candles for my store, and just happened to be a billionaire, had bought her grandmother's old property here in Sweet River. The plantation-style house had looked like something out of a horror film the last time I'd seen it.

But with Jasmine's money, determination, and the ability

to have crews working twenty-four-seven, I wasn't surprised the house had gone from a horror movie to something fabulous in just three months.

"I can't wait."

I blinked. The back door was open to the bakery. "Is Lizzie there with you?"

"Yeah. We're all here. Why?"

George did that weird whine that happened whenever something was wrong.

"Ainsley? Where are you?" Shannon asked. "Why is George whining like that? Are you safe? Remember our code word?" We had that word in case we were kidnapped but I couldn't for the life of me remember what it was.

"Ask Lizzie if her assistant is working tonight."

"I'm putting you on speaker. Ainsley needs to know if someone is working at the bakery tonight."

"No. She should have gone home by now," Lizzie said. There was hesitation in her voice. "What's going on?"

"The back door is open and it's dark inside."

"Oh. No. Do you think someone broke in? Or maybe it's that door. It sticks sometimes; maybe she didn't lock it when she left."

I stood outside the bakery. "Hello?"

"Ains, I'm texting your brother," Shannon said. "Do not go in there alone."

"Don't!" That may have come out harsher than I meant. "Maybe, the door just didn't shut properly. It happens with these old buildings. No reason to sound the alarm. He'll kill me if nothing is going on."

Though, my own alarm system—George—let out a low

growl.

I cleared my throat. "Hello?"

"What do you see?" Shannon asked. "And I don't care what you say, I'm texting Greg."

"It's dark."

"The light panel is right inside the door," Lizzie said anxiously. "I don't keep any money there. I don't know why someone would break in. It has to be the door didn't shut right. I'm sure everything is fine."

I wanted to believe her, but my dog was saying otherwise. A shiver slid down my spine.

"George, sit." I reached my arm in to hit the lights.

I finally found the switch. Slightly blinded by the flash of lights, it took a minute for my eyes to adjust.

I didn't see anything from the doorway, but George still growled. "Hello?"

I stepped a few feet into the bakery and looked down.

Crud. I wished I hadn't done that. Acid burned in the back of my throat.

"Ainsley? Say something," Shannon said.

"Someone call my brother," I whispered. What if the killer was still here? I glanced around so fast, my head started spinning.

Or maybe it was all the blood. I closed my eyes and took a deep breath.

Big mistake. The coppery scent filled my nose.

"There's a dead body on the floor." Other than it looked like a man, I couldn't tell much since the person had fallen face down.

"Hey, that's not funny," Lizzie said angrily. "I don't like

jokes that are mean."

"I'm not joking."

"George, stay." I put my hand up. He whined shrilly but did what I asked. Him trampling on a crime scene wasn't the best idea.

I took another step inside.

"Oh. No."

"Ainsley? Ainsley? Are you okay?"

Chapter Two

THERE WAS SO much blood in the back of the bakery and my stomach launched into my throat. I grabbed a cabinet handle to balance myself.

Darn. I'm not supposed to touch anything. I'd been at enough crime scenes to know better.

A muffled sound came from the corner.

"Ainsley, I swear if you don't tell me you're okay, I'm going to kill you the next time I see you," Shannon said angrily.

"I'm fine. There's a body and a lot of blood. And I just heard a noise."

"Greg is thirty seconds away. What if the killer is hiding?" She whispered this time. She'd helped me with enough cases that we had begun to think the same way.

"It was a moan. At least, I think it was. Someone might need help. It's coming from the freezer."

"Ainsley, no," Shannon said. "Greg will be there in seconds. Just back out of the bakery."

But if someone was hurt, I had to help.

There was another moan and then a shrill scream that reverberated through my body. I held my breath as I carefully stepped around the body to the freezer.

Please don't be the killer. Please don't be the killer.

I had to force myself to pull the lever toward me slowly.

I blinked again, as a cold blast hit my face. The sight inside was more than I could bear.

"Noooo," I cried out.

A hand touched my shoulder. Three things happened at once. I screamed. I dropped my phone in the blood on the floor.

And I might have peed myself a little.

"It's me," Greg said softly.

My hands shook as my brother turned me around to face him.

"She's dead," I cried out. "Greg. Help her."

Someone pushed past him. "My men are here. We need to get out of the way."

"No. What if she's dead?" Tears streamed down my face. Greg put my arm around his neck and half drug me the long way around the large island in the middle of the kitchen. I'm sure he did it to keep from trampling the crime scene.

As we stepped outside, a breeze hit my face and I took a big breath.

EMTs ran past us.

Everything on my body shook.

"Why is it so cold?"

It was late June in Texas, but my hands were freezing.

"Stay here," Greg ordered. "I'll be right back."

"Kevin, get her a blanket and something warm to drink. I'm pretty sure she's in shock."

I shook my head. "I'm fine. I have to know if she's alive."

"Who?" Kevin asked.

"Mrs. Whedon," I sobbed. "She's in the freezer."

"You aren't fine," Greg yelled. He did that when he was scared. But why was he scared? "You have no color in your face and you're shaking."

"Find out if she's alive, and I'll go."

My brother, who happens to be the sheriff, grunted. "Deputy, stay with her," he said to Kevin, who usually ran the front desk and had an aversion to blood.

George nudged me with his big cold nose, and I bent down to wrap my arms around him. It was as if he understood my insides were jelly and he was sorry that he'd found yet another dead body. He rested his head on my shoulder.

One of the officers came out and called for a bus. While I'm not up on the latest cop-speak, I understood that meant an ambulance. That had to mean she was alive. Good. Good. If she was alive, there was hope.

George snuggled closer and it was a good thing I'd been holding on to him. The next thing I knew, my butt hit the hard concrete and my back was against the brick wall. My dog lay down and put his head in my lap.

Greg might have been right. I wasn't feeling so good. My stomach churned and a tight band squeezed the top of my head. My teeth chattered I was so cold.

Kevin had knelt down and was talking to me, but I couldn't comprehend what he was saying.

I tried to tell him, but my mouth wouldn't work.

Then someone scooped me up from the ground.

I turned my head to find Jake, my boyfriend and favorite person in the world, staring at me with concern. He sat me inside his truck and then went about checking my pulse. He put something on my finger. There were so many people around that I hadn't noticed before and then Jake was waving a hand in front of my face.

He was saying something but it was like one of those dreams where you're going to win a million dollars and all you have to do is talk to the person on the phone but you can't understand what they are saying.

Or maybe that just happens in my dreams.

He took my face in his hands. "You're in shock. We're going to the hospital," he said.

Before I could answer he shut the door. He opened the driver side, and helped George into the back part of the cab, before getting behind the wheel.

"No," I managed to say. It was as if I could think the words, but I couldn't get them to come out of my mouth.

"Ainsley, you're in severe shock. Your pulse is through the roof. You're turning grayer by the minute and your lips are blue. I understand that you hate hospitals, but you need oxygen and to warm up quickly."

"Head hurts." It did, so much that I had to close my eyes even though it was dark outside.

"Another symptom. You're going to be fine but there's no discussion about the hospital." He sounded scared.

Why is everyone so scared? I'm the one who found the dead body.

I sighed. It was too difficult to say words out loud. The pain in my head intensified and there were tiny sparks in my eyes. A nap. I really needed a nap.

Jake was yelling and George started barking, but I was so sleepy.

When I woke up, there were a lot of bright lights and it was finally warm. But someone had driven a railroad spike through my head. I had to close my eyes again.

"Jake." My throat was dry and sore.

"She's awake," someone said. "Jake's just outside. Can you tell me if anything hurts?"

Words still seemed so hard. So I pointed to my head. A mask was placed on my face, and there was a prick on my hand.

"Dim the lights," the voice said. "Ainsley, I'm Dr. Kline. I want you to blink if you understand me."

My eyelids felt like fifty-pound weights but I blinked.

"Good. Your blood pressure is high. That's what's causing the pain in your head. We've given you something for that. You will be fine—Jake brought you in fast enough for us to stop what was happening. The medicine will make you sleepy. Don't fight it. The quickest way to heal is to sleep."

I didn't have a choice—the darkness was already swallowing me whole.

"Ainsley McGregor, you need to wake up so I can murder you," Shannon said. "Jake, the doctor said she should be awake right now."

"My sister never does the expected," Greg chimed in.

"Rest is important," Jake said firmly. "She had a big shock." His large hand squeezed mine.

Why was everyone in my room? And what was the shock?

The blood. The body.

I sat up straight gasping for air.

Shannon screamed.

I forced my eyes to open, as big arms wrapped around me. "You're okay, Ainsley," Jake said calmly. "You're in the hospital. You went into shock last night. But your vitals are good. They gave you some drugs for your blood pressure and migraine, which made you sleepy. But you're fine."

I wasn't sure if he was reassuring me or himself.

Shannon started laughing. "I'm so sorry I screamed. You scared the toot out of me," she said. And then her arms were around me as well. "I've been so scared. Jake said you were very sick last night. When you didn't answer my 137 calls, I was worried you were dead."

"Water," I croaked. Swallowing gravel might have been easier than talking.

Jake put a straw to my lips and the cold water was such a relief. Then he raised the head of the bed so I could lean back.

"George?" I stared at Jake.

He smiled. "He's with Mike at the winery." Mike was Shannon's husband and one of George's favorite humans.

"What happened?" I whispered hoarsely.

"A lot," Shannon said, and then cut her eyes to Greg.

"What did you do?" I asked.

He sighed. "I brought your friend Lizzie in for questioning. For the record, she was much more concerned for you than she was the victim in her bakery."

My brain was still fuzzy and his words didn't make sense. "Lizzie was with Shannon."

"That's what I said," my friend commented. "She was with us the whole time. There's no way she could have killed him."

They thought Lizzie killed someone? It wasn't possible. She was the kindest soul I'd ever met and treated everyone who walked in her shop as a long-lost friend she was happy to see.

I rubbed my head.

"That's it. You two are out of here," Jake said firmly. I'd never seen him so angry. "The last thing she needs right now is to get upset again. You both know better."

"Sorry," Shannon said. "Please don't make me leave. I won't talk about it."

"When did you get so bossy?" I asked. My throat hurt but not quite as bad as it did before the water.

Greg nodded. "I'll go check with the doctor to see if we can get you checked out. You'll rest better at home."

"Wait." I held up my left hand and then I closed my eyes and flashes of the scene the night before zoomed through my brain. "Mrs. Whedon. Is she okay?"

I opened my eyes to find Greg, Shannon, and Jake all staring at one another.

"What's going on? Tell me."

A tear slid down Shannon's cheek.

Oh. No. This wasn't good.

Chapter Three

M Y BROTHER, BEST friend, and the man I loved, refused to tell me anything. They all just stood around my hospital bed staring at the floor.

"Tell me. Making me worry isn't going to help. You said you aren't supposed to stress me out."

Jake took a deep breath. "Ainsley, I don't think you understand what just happened to you. Severe shock can shut down your organs."

"If Jake hadn't brought you in, it might have been really bad," Greg said.

They were ignoring my question.

"Shannon. Tell me what is going on."

She glanced up at Jake, who shook his head.

"I'm stressing out more not knowing. Just tell me. This is ridiculous." My voice was shrill and not at all like me. I swung my legs over to the side of the bed, determined to find out what happened.

My vision blurred and I had to close my eyes again. It didn't keep me from yelling at them. "I don't know why I went into shock last night. As you all know, it wasn't my first time to run into something like that. But I need to know the truth. And I need to know it now."

"I promised," Shannon said, as she glanced at Jake again.

"Jake, I love you, but someone better tell me the truth. If I didn't think I could handle it, I wouldn't have asked."

"Gran, I mean, Mrs. Whedon, and Becky, Lizzie's assistant baker, were both in the freezer at the bakery. The doctors say you saved their lives."

Thank goodness. Gran was alive. I searched through my memories of the previous night, but I didn't remember seeing the assistant. "Is Becky okay?"

Shannon nodded. "She was released from the hospital last night."

"I don't understand why Gran was there." She was in her eighties and I could have sworn she had a date with the judge last night.

Though, most of yesterday and last night was still a jumble in my brain.

We'd been talking about the float. They all went home, and then I took George for a walk.

"We're not sure," Greg said. "We're still trying to put a timeline together."

"Why can't you just ask her?" As soon as I said the words, my stomach churned. Tears burned as they fell to my cheeks. "You said she's alive. Did you lie?" That last bit came out as a croak.

"She's in a coma," Jake said quickly. "She took a pretty good whack to the head. The doctors think she'll be fine, but she is older. They don't know what state she'll be in when she wakes up. The extent of her injuries can't be fully addressed until she's lucid."

But she's alive.

Gran was the toughest woman I'd ever met. If she was

alive, she'd be fighting. I believed that with my whole soul.

"I need to see her. Now."

Once again, they all looked at one another.

I cocked my head in much the same way George does when he thinks I'm acting weird.

"We'll make it happen," Jake said.

Shannon helped me dress. Jake had been thoughtful enough to bring me a clean T-shirt, jeans, and sneakers. Not long after Shannon braided my curly hair, I signed the discharge papers. I was more embarrassed than anything. It wasn't like I'd never seen a dead body or blood before.

It was all so weird.

"You'll have to ride in one of these," Jake said as he pushed a wheelchair in.

I shook my head.

"Hospital policy," the nurse said coming in behind him. "The doctor asked if you could stay put for five minutes. She's finishing with a patient and wants to speak with you before you go."

"I really need to see a friend of mine. Can it wait?"

The nurse shook her head. "She wants to talk to about your condition."

Jake and Shannon whipped around.

"My condition?" Was I dying? Is that why I went into shock? My heart beat double-time and my palms sweated.

Stop being so dramatic. I closed my eyes and forced myself to calm down.

"The doctor will explain." Then she handed me the discharge papers and left.

"Ains, is there something you need to tell us?" Shannon

asked. "Well, maybe, Jake first and then me right after?" She smiled.

My brain was still slow and I had no idea what she was talking about. Jake had a weird smile on his face. "What? I don't understand."

Shannon laughed.

The doctor came in holding a folder. She was dressed in scrubs and was short. With her close-cropped pixyish hair, she reminded me of an elf.

"Hi, Ainsley, good to see you up and around. I'm Dr. Kline. I treated you when you came in."

"Hi, and thank you." I was so woozy when I came in that I didn't remember much. I reached out and Jake took my hand, giving me strength for whatever was to come.

"You're, welcome. There is something I need to discuss with you before you go." She stared pointedly at Jake and Shannon.

"It's okay. They're family," I said. I didn't want to be alone if it was bad news.

"Your brother explained what you saw last night. But he says that usually doesn't bother you."

I nodded. Though, it always bothered me, and often haunted me in my nightmares.

"In the past few weeks have you felt light-headed or dizzy?"

"Yes, she has," Jake answered for me. "Remember when you got up off the couch the other night? You were dizzy."

"And tired," Shannon added. "She's been very tired lately."

"Right. That all makes sense. I ran several blood tests and

your blood sugars were very low when you came in. I'm curious what you ate yesterday, if you can remember."

"She had an iced dirty chai latte and a chocolate chip muffin for breakfast," Shannon said. I'd stopped for my regular on the way into the shop.

The doctor looked from her to me, and I nodded.

"And for lunch?"

"Um. I fed George, my dog, and then we got really busy at the store. We had a meeting after we closed, and I ate more cookies from the bakery than I should have because I was hungry. I usually don't miss meals. I was meeting my friends that night and we always have a ton a food, so I wasn't really worried about it."

"Right. I thought that might be the case. It makes sense."

Not to me, but I was curious about this condition. She didn't seem worried, so, I'd crossed imminent death off my list.

Jake squeezed my hand and I glanced up at him. He smiled, not looking upset or anything. Maybe he knew what was wrong.

"What's likely happening is your diet is sending your sugars up too high, and then you're crashing. And when you don't eat, that's just as bad for someone who is hypoglycemic."

"I don't normally go without meals," I repeated, and then smiled.

"That's good. I brought this folder for you. You need to keep an eye on your sugar intake. You don't have to give anything up, just not quite as much sugar as you ingested yesterday, and you need to eat protein every few hours to keep those levels even. It's not a big deal at all, you just have to make sure you're taking care of yourself."

She handed me the folder. "It's important to get this under control for many reasons. We've seen links to diabetes, and if your sugars are too low or too high, it can affect your organs."

"I—uh. This sounds like a big deal to me."

She smiled. "You will be fine. That's why I put this folder together with tips for you to keep those sugars where they need to be. It's possible that you crashed, and that, combined with what you saw, which I understand was gruesome, was the perfect storm.

"You seem to have a good support system, so I suggest you all read the items in the folder. You didn't have a primary care physician listed in your records. You're welcome to come see me." She handed me a card. "But no matter what, you'll need to see someone in the next month for some blood tests."

After she left, Greg walked back in.

"Why are you all staring at the door?"

"The doc was just here. Ains has hypo something," Shannon said. "She can't eat cake for breakfast anymore."

I frowned.

Jake chuckled. "She can, as long as she eats eggs too."

"Ewwww," I said.

Greg gave us his *you people are weird* stare. "I have no idea what you guys are talking about. But I did get you on the list, as well as everyone on the shop, for visitation rights to see Gran, I mean, Mrs. Whedon," he said.

I'd wondered where he'd been. "Thanks."

"She's still in ICU, and the nurse said only one person at a time."

Jake wheeled me down the hall to Mrs. Whedon's room. Someone had put an afghan across the hospital blankets. It was in her signature avocado.

Peggy, Don's wife and one of the loveliest souls in Sweet River, sat beside the bed doing some sort of needlework and chatting as if she and Mrs. Whedon were having a conversation.

She glanced up and smiled. "Well, look at that. Jake is pushing our Ainsley in a wheelchair."

"Hi," I said.

Peggy waved us up to the bed. Gran had so many bandages on her head, it almost looked like a turban. And she was so pale against the pillow.

I swallowed hard. The last thing she needed was me blubbering.

"Jake, why don't we give them a minute," Peggy said. "You go on and talk to her, Ainsley. The doctors say it's good. There's a chance she's listening but just can't wake up yet."

I nodded, unable to say anything because there was a giant frog in my throat and tears streamed down my cheeks.

The door shut softly, and I took her cold hand in mine.

"I need you to get well. Do you hear me, Gran? I can't lose you."

I leaned down and kissed her knobby fingers. She didn't need me sobbing like a child. I took some tissues from the side table by the bed and cleaned up my face.

"Sorry. I'm used to you bouncing around and telling me

what to do with my life. It's weird to see you still and quiet. That only happens when you're mad most of the time. But here's the deal. You get well, and I'll find the person who did this to you.

"We're going to make them pay, Gran. I promise you that. Nobody hurts my family."

Chapter Four

THE NEXT MORNING, after a breakfast of eggs and bacon, which Jake had made me, I set off for town. I had a cooler bag full of healthy lunch and snack items he'd put together. And instructions that he would text me every few hours to make sure I was taking care of myself.

If they need a king for the Mother Hen Club, he would totally win.

My first stop was the hospital.

I sat with Gran telling her about all the snacks, and how he'd deemed himself my new chef and nutritionist. I might have been offended, but it all came from love. He was so worried about losing me, and it was just beyond sweet. It had taken a great deal of coercing to convince him to let me drive myself into town.

When Maria, Carrie's mom, showed up, I left to give my brother the grand inquisition he deserved. He'd refused to take my calls the night before. As my brain came back online, I had a list of questions.

Greg texted Jake and said he was busy working the case. That was my brother's code for: *Stay out of it, Ainsley.*

Jake wasn't particularly helpful, since he too felt I should stay out of things and rest as much as possible. He wanted me to stay home today, but I was fine. And I had to find out what happened.

It was like they didn't even know me.

Greg couldn't avoid me if I was standing in front of his desk.

"Morning, Ainsley." Kevin was at the front counter, which is where Greg liked to keep him. He was a nice guy but his skills as a deputy were questionable.

I waved as I passed by. If I asked for permission, Greg would make some excuse not to see me. His light was on, so I soldiered on.

I sat down in the chair in front of my brother's desk, while he typed on a computer and tried to ignore me. I'd learned one of his tricks, though: the silent game. The longer the silence went on, the bigger the chance that someone would say something. He used it on suspects and criminals all the time.

He sighed. "Fine. What do you want?"

"To know who tried to kill Gran."

"You know I can't comment on an ongoing investigation."

"You brought Lizzie in for questioning. Tell me why."

"I told you she isn't a suspect at the moment. She was with your friends, but Kane is still working on time of death. And with him, everything has to be exactly perfect numbers wise before he'll even hint at what it is. Lizzie was familiar with the murdered man. We have no suspects right now."

"You know I'm going to ask her exactly what she said to you. Why not tell me?"

He squinted and then rubbed his forehead. More than once he'd blamed my incessant questions for a headache. He had no idea how far I'd go this time.

Someone had hurt Gran. I wasn't into vendettas, but harming an old woman was a no-brainer when it came to making people pay.

"You can at least tell me who the dead man is. It will be announced in the paper tomorrow. I heard the nurses talking at the hospital this morning."

"Morton Gallagher. He was your friend Lizzie's ex-husband."

I didn't know Lizzie had been married.

"Do you have any other info? And why would someone want to kill him?"

"That would be why we brought her in and asked the same thing."

I sat and stared at him.

"I know what you're doing."

"Waiting?" I smiled sweetly.

"Since you were one of the victims, I have to keep you out of this." Greg leaned forward on his elbows. "It has to be by the book."

"I understand," I whispered. "But he put one of my favorite humans in a coma, Greg. You and Jake are both calling her Gran, as well. She's family. I'm not going to sit around and wait for whoever it was to come back and finish off the job."

He frowned. "The killer is probably long gone by now. They'd be an idiot to stick around town."

"I don't see it that way. There are possible witnesses who saw the killer. Why would they leave them alive? And did that look like a professional killer to you? My brain is still hazy about what I saw but there was a lot of blood, and his head was bashed in pretty good. What did the killer use? I don't remember seeing anything."

Greg leaned back in his chair. "A large iron skillet. Kane says the victim didn't die from the first blow, but it appears he hit that steel table on his way down, and it cracked the skull into several pieces."

Gross. The churning in my stomach intensified. I hadn't been worried about anything until I'd spoken my fears out loud. What if the killer hung around? Had they seen me go in the bakery that night?

"Did Mrs. Whedon get hit with the pan?"

He shook his head. "Kane says it looks like she was pushed into the freezer, and tripped over Becky. As she was going down, she hit her head on the marble slab in there."

That slab was what Lizzie rolled out her pies and cookies on. She said it helped the dough stay more pliable, for longer.

"What about Becky?"

"We interviewed her at the hospital. She'd gone back to the bakery because she wanted to get everything ready for the next day. That way she could sleep in a little longer.

"At least, that's what she said. She can't remember if she locked the back door. She remembers someone grabbed her and she screamed. That's it. Until she woke up and found Mrs. Whedon on top of her and freaked out. It took two EMTs and three of my men to get her to calm down."

"Who wouldn't freak out if they woke up with a body on top of them in a freezer? Did she have a head injury?"

He nodded. "Lucky for her, she hit the shelving in the

freezer, so her injuries weren't as bad. We thought she might be faking the amnesia, but the psychiatrist says it's common with that sort of head injury. She hit the shelf right at the temple. As for Lizzie's ex, between the heavy frying pan and the ledge of that hard steel table, he didn't have a chance."

I shivered. What a horrible way to die. At least Becky was okay. She was a sweet girl and always so cheerful. Since Mrs. Whedon couldn't talk, Becky would be my next stop. Maybe she'd remember something she'd forgotten to tell the police.

"I see those wheels turning. I told you all of this so you can see we are working with the case. We don't need any interference. And there are rules about you being involved."

"Yes, but technically, I'm not a victim. So, there's that."

"Do you remember seeing anyone before you walked in? Maybe just outside the bakery?"

I shook my head, and then it hit me.

"What? You have that look, Ains."

"I took George for a walk. A jogger ran past us and my dog went berserk. Like, nearly pulled my arm out of the socket because he was trying to get that person. He's usually friendly with strangers. It was weird."

Greg grabbed a pen off the desk. "Where is George?"

"He's hanging out with Jake at his place. He'll bring him in when his shift starts. I stopped by the hospital first to see Gran, and he's not allowed in there."

"That reminds me, what happened to George the night I passed out? There's no way Jake left him in the truck."

"Don't you remember asking about that before? But you're off topic," he said. "You saw a man. Tell me about it."

I stared at him. It wasn't that I was playing any sort of

game, I just couldn't remember any details. The night was still a blur.

"Jake took him into the hospital. It caused quite the uproar from what I understand. But no one could pull your dog or Jake away from you, until Mike showed up. It's a good thing he's strong."

I smiled. Awww. My guys really loved me.

"Focus, Ains. I have no leads right now. Anything you could tell me would be helpful. Close your eyes and run me through what you saw."

I'd done this more than a dozen times with people I'd interviewed. And Greg had done it to me way more than that. Trouble always seemed to find me.

After a deep breath, I closed my eyes.

"Look at your paper. You're harshing my brain vibe."

He snorted. "How do you do that?"

"You give off an intense vibe," I said.

I tried to focus again. "It's dark in that part of the park and the person ran fast. The big trees hide the streetlamps and it's hard to see much of anything but shadows. George likes doing his business there because he thinks no one can see him." I wouldn't have been in that area if George hadn't been with me.

Greg snorted.

"Didn't the cameras from the park or Lizzie's security system see something?"

He shook his head. "That row of magnolia trees the mayor insisted on block the one camera we have at the park that faces that way. And Lizzie's system only works when she arms it."

My phone buzzed in my pocket. "Oh, thanks for my new phone," I said. It had been waiting on the kitchen bar downstairs this morning. "I'm not sure how you were able to transfer all my contacts without my password, but thanks."

"You're welcome." I guess he wasn't going to explain how he'd done that. "Come on. Stop stalling—I need info."

I rolled my eyes, though they were still closed so he didn't see. "Fine." I took a deep breath again. "Air on my face, the person was so close. Maybe they didn't see George until he lunged. He was barking like crazy and I was embarrassed. I was more focused on making him calm down."

"Think. Maybe you saw something out of the corner of your eye."

I had glanced that way to see what my dog was going nuts over. "Black ball cap. Short hair, or it was tucked underneath. Black short-sleeve T-shirt but I can only see the end of the sleeve to the elbow. I think it's a man, but I'm not sure."

"That's good. How tall?"

"Over six feet. Jake's height maybe."

I moved my eyes down. Oh. My eyes popped open.

"What is it? What do you see?"

"Jeans," I said. "Not a jogger."

Greg sat back. "But maybe a killer running from a crime scene."

A shiver ran down my spine again, and not the good kind that Jake gives me whenever he kisses me.

"Yep."

Chapter Five

Finding the one witness who was conscious, besides me, wasn't easy. It didn't help that I had no idea where Becky lived. I drove by the bakery, which was closed. It always was on Sunday and Monday, but I wondered when Lizzie would open for business again. There had been quite the mess in the back of that bakery, and she might be mourning her ex-husband.

The one she'd never mentioned.

I pulled in behind Shannon's coffee shop. Since she and Mike had married, she lived full-time out at the winery. Lizzie rented the apartment upstairs now. It was a convenient arrangement since the bakery was only a little ways down from it.

I climbed the stairs, and then knocked on the door.

"Just a minute," Lizzie said.

When she opened the door, it was obvious she'd been crying, and she was covered in flour. "Oh, thank goodness you're okay. I was going to come to see you this afternoon, but look at you out and about." She glanced around behind me, as if she were looking for someone, and then pulled me inside. After shutting the door, she locked it.

That wasn't something most of us did here in Sweet River. There wasn't much of a need. Though, after everything that happened, her nervousness was understandable.

"How are you?" she said, as I followed her to the sofa.

"I'm fine. Shannon told me you guys were there waiting for me to wake up, but that Greg told you to leave."

She shook her head. "He wasn't mean. We were at the hospital and Jake promised us that you were okay. Shannon went home to check on George. He was quite the famous guy at the hospital.

"Greg asked if we could have an informal conversation, and if I would come down to the station the next morning. I was frazzled. Becky was doing better and I'd offered to drive her home, but she'd called her parents. I'm sorry for everyone involved. Truly. You have to know that. I don't understand why he was there or—your brother took me to the bakery. His body was gone but the blood. Oh. Ainsley, it's all just too much."

She put her head in her hands. "I wished I'd stayed with you and never walked back into the bakery. I will never get that image out of my head."

I frowned. Usually, Greg had a cleanup crew who took care of the blood and any evidence of a crime once forensics had what they needed.

That he'd forced her to go in there—my fists tightened. He wanted to see how she would react. It was manipulative and unnecessary. My brother and I would be having words.

"I'm not sure I'll ever get the sight of all that blood out of my mind. The very idea of going back to bake in there turns my stomach. I love that place, but now..."

"I can imagine," I said.

She shook her head. "Of course, none of that is as bad as

what happened to you, Mrs. Whedon and my poor Becky. Have you heard any news about Mrs. Whedon? I've gone up a few times to check on her, but no one will tell me anything."

Lizzie always seemed so cheerful and chill, but she was wringing her hands.

"I'm fine. It was a blood sugar thing, which you probably heard from Shannon. And Gran is holding steady. I'm sure she's just staying in that coma so that we'll all worry about her."

"I'll feel better when she wakes up," Lizzie said, and then pulled a throw pillow toward her stomach. "We all will."

"Are you okay?" I asked. "That was your ex, who was murdered." I didn't mention the part about her never telling any of us about him.

She blew out a breath. "I—it's so confusing. He'd mentioned he was coming to town on Sunday. I don't know what he was doing here early, or in my bakery on Friday night. I've been racking my brain trying to remember our last conversation."

"Were you close?"

She shrugged. "We've been divorced for ten years. We were teens and…it wasn't a happy marriage. He couldn't keep it in his pants. I knew he was cheating on me but I was young and dumb. He had a great job working with his dad, and we had a nice house. That's when I taught myself how to bake—you know, to keep my mind off things."

"When I turned twenty-one, he came in one day and said he was gay."

"Oh." I did not see that coming.

"Oh, is right. He felt so guilty about deceiving me that he gave me all the proceeds from selling the house and insisted on paying alimony."

"That must have been a rough time for you."

She bit her lip. "It was and it wasn't. I was so relieved that his going out at all hours wasn't really my fault. I thought I was a complete failure as a wife. I think a little bit of that doubt is still in my subconscious somewhere and that's why I never date. I say it's about work, but I'm not sure sometimes."

I used to be the same way until I met Jake. Work had always come first because men were a constant disappointment. Until Jake.

"It took about a year and half, but we became great friends. We did have a lot in common and we even went on vacations together through the years." She sobbed.

I scooched forward so I could wrap my arms around her. She cried on my shoulder for a few minutes. When she pulled away, she grabbed several tissues from the box on the coffee table.

"I'm a mess. Just before you got here, it sort of hit me that he's really gone. We've been in each other's lives since we were in elementary school. We grew up together." She pushed the wad of tissues to her nose.

"I'm sorry for your loss."

"Thank you. I feel guilty about him dying in my shop. What if he was just stopping by to tell me he was early, and a robber killed him?"

"Is that what the police think happened?" I didn't want her to know I'd spent the last hour with Greg.

She shook her head. "I have no idea what's going on or what they think happened. Greg is great but he was pretty hard on me. And I felt kind of dumb because I had no answers. I'm so confused. And Morton's mom will probably have me killed in my sleep. She will blame me for this. She hates me."

She cried again. "I loved him. I wouldn't hurt him. He's been such a great friend to me through the years. He's the one who encouraged me to work at bakeries all over the country, so I could hone my craft. And he pushed me to open up my own when he thought I was ready."

"Why would his mom think you had something to do with it?" After I said it, I realized how rude the question was.

"His mom thinks I turned him gay. Can you imagine? Every time she sees me, she makes an offhand comment like, 'If you'd been a better wife, he wouldn't have turned to the other side.' As. If."

"Um." The idiocy of people never failed to surprise me.

"Right? Like I had a choice in the matter. I swear the only reason he came out was because he knew how miserable he was making me. I think he half thought I would stay with him so he didn't have to tell his parents. But his mom couldn't be mad at him. He is her—or was her—little pumpkin. So all the blame went to me."

"I'm sure Greg brought this up, but what if it wasn't a robbery? Since you two were close, do you know if he had people who were angry with him? Anything to do with his work, maybe?"

She sighed. "He said he needed to talk to me about something. He was working through a problem, but I don't know if it was relationship stuff or work. Like I said, I've known him a long time and we are each other's sounding boards."

She hugged herself and leaned back on the couch. "I can't believe he's gone. My heart actually hurts. Our past sounds like something out of a soap opera, but except for that short time after the divorce, we've always been best friends. If he hadn't pushed me, I would have never realized my dreams of owning my bakery."

Lizzie sat up straighter. "Ainsley, Shannon explained how you're a world-class detective. I need to know who did this to him, and who hurt our favorite grump, Mrs. Whedon. I'll help in any way I can."

I smiled, and then put a hand on top of hers. "World class is quite a stretch. I'm nosy, and I like following clues. I'll be honest, I'm lucky most of the time. But I would do this whether you asked or not, because they hurt someone I love, too."

She nodded. "Tell me what you need."

"Let's start with Becky's address." I had some questions for the only witness who could tell me what happened.

A HALF HOUR later we pulled up in front of the apartment building directly across from the college. I was familiar with the building, as several of my students lived here during the school year.

It had good security, it was well kept and cheap, just the kind of place parents felt safe dropping their kids off for their first year. It was a huge complex with several buildings and it basically served as a dorm, as the college had limited space for on-campus living.

"I had no idea this place was so big," Lizzie said. She'd insisted on coming with me. Since the incident, she hadn't been able to get in touch with Becky and she was worried about her.

I explained to her about it basically acting like a dorm for the school, but others lived there as well.

"It looks like she's on the second floor," I said.

Lizzie knocked on the door.

No one answered.

She knocked again.

Nothing.

The door next to Becky's opened a small crack. "What do you want?"

"It's Lizzie, Becky's boss. I just wanted to check on her."

"She's not here," the voice said. "I haven't seen her. I told the cops I didn't know where she was."

I frowned. Greg hadn't said anything about following up. Though, he wasn't telling me everything.

"Do you know where she is?"

"You're strangers. I'm not sharing anything. Maybe she's with her boyfriend or something. Now, go away."

I glanced at Lizzie, who seemed confused.

"Okay, thanks. If she comes home, can you ask her to call Lizzie? We just want to make sure she's okay."

The girl slammed the door.

"I take it you had no idea about the boyfriend?"

She shook her head. "It's strange that she never mentioned him, and I've never seen anyone around the shop. But now I'm scared."

"Why?" I asked as we headed downstairs.

"She is never without her phone. It's my only complaint about her work ethic. What if the killer has kidnapped her?"

I stopped at the end of the stairs. "Greg said that was unlikely. He thinks the killer is probably long gone."

"Probably?"

Since I couldn't convince myself, I didn't bother forcing the issue.

"And that isn't usually how it works. Like murderers don't normally do kidnappings. Normally. I think it's more likely she's scared and hiding out somewhere."

At least, I hoped so.

"We need to find the boyfriend. Was he there that night? Are you sure you can't remember anyone hanging around the shop and talking to her?"

We moved toward the car, and then she stopped. I almost ran into her.

"What is it?"

She turned to face me. "I can't lose her too, Ainsley. I've only known her for five months, but I adore her. She's like the little sister I never had. If anything happens to her, I just—can't."

I wrapped my arms around her and gave her a hug. I'd never been much of a hugger—that is until I moved to Sweet River. People in Texas were fond of hugs.

"We'll find her. I'm sure she's okay," I lied. I was, however, hoping very hard she was just scared and hiding out somewhere. "How about her home? Do her parents live nearby?"

"They have a ranch in Round Top."

I squeezed her again, and then let go.

"Well, I know where we will be having lunch. But if we don't stop and pick up Shannon and Jasmine, they will never forgive us."

"I don't feel much like eating," Lizzie said.

"Trust me, you will when you walk into the restaurant. Then we'll go find Becky's mom and dad."

Lunch with the girls would help take her mind off of things.

I just prayed we found the adorable Becky alive.

Chapter Six

AN HOUR LATER, Shannon, Jasmine, Lizzie, and I were finishing our meal at Teague's Tavern. It was good to get out of town for a bit and this was one of my favorite restaurants ever.

Life was just better after some shrimp and bacon grits, and I was proud that I said no to the molten chocolate cake. I mean, the grits probably weren't the best for blood sugar and I didn't want to push it. I didn't have time to pass out today.

"Can I get anything else for you, ma'am?" the waiter asked. It always made me feel so old when people said ma'am, but it was another one of those Texas things.

"We're good. You wouldn't by chance know where the Relehan ranch is do you?"

"No, ma'am. I can ask the boss. He pretty much knows everyone around here."

"Thanks, I'd appreciate it."

A few minutes later, Don Teague—the owner—came out and waved hello. We'd met him a couple of times. Shannon and I always ate here when we went shopping in Round Top, which was a lot. And it was also our favorite place to double-date with our guys.

"Ainsley and Shannon, it's good to see you again." He

shook my hand and then Shannon's. "I see you brought some friends. Thank you for that."

I smiled. He'd been a news guy and had traveled the world, but he was as friendly as they came.

"These are our friends Jasmine and Lizzie."

They waved and said hello.

"Todd says you need to know where the Relehan ranch is. I don't normally give away personal information about my customers."

I explained the situation.

"You're on the case? That last one you solved was a doozy. You should write a book or something."

I snorted. My brother still thought I was writing one. That was my excuse for being so nosy about his investigations. Every once in a while he'd say, "How's that book going?" And I'd just nod, like things were good.

"We are worried about Becky. She works for Lizzie and she hasn't been answering her phone. The poor girl had such an awful experience on Friday night, and we're her friends, as well."

"Please." Lizzie had the best puppy dog eyes I'd ever seen. I would never be able to tell her no.

"All right," he said. "Let me make a call. I'll be right back." He left and we settled our tab with Todd.

Then Don came back. "I wrote down the directions for you. I called out there but no one answered. It's Sunday, so they might be in the pool out back or in the barn. They love their horses."

"Thanks." I picked up the paper, and soon we were on our way. The great thing about Round Top is it doesn't take long to get anywhere. We pulled up the long dirt road about five minutes later.

"So, barn or house?"

"Let's try the barn," Shannon said. "If she's a horse girl, and she's upset, that's the first place to look."

It seemed a bit odd to snoop around private property, but it wasn't like Shannon and I hadn't done this before.

We found Becky, and the tight band that had been around my chest let go. It was like I could breathe for the first time in hours.

She was in khaki shorts and rubber boots, cleaning out one of the stalls.

"Becky," Lizzie called out. But she didn't acknowledge us. "Becky," she said again. That's when I noticed the AirPods in her ears.

I pointed and Lizzie nodded. She walked over to the stall and was about to touch her on the shoulder when Becky screamed and turned around with the pitchfork pointed at Lizzie.

All the color drained from the poor girl's face.

"It's me, Becky. I'm sorry I startled you," Lizzie said. It was a good thing she was fast on her feet or she might have been wearing that pitchfork.

"I—" Then Becky sobbed. Poor thing. After everything she'd been through, we snuck up on her and scared her to death.

Lizzie took the pitchfork from her hands and set it against the stall wall. Then she took the girl in her arms.

"I'm sorry," Becky said, as she took the AirPods out of her ears. "You scared the pee out of me."

Lizzie smiled. "I didn't mean to but you couldn't hear us. I wanted to make sure you're okay. You haven't been answering your phone."

"Oh. I turned it off because some reporter kept trying to call me. I just turned it back on so I could listen to music. I did text you back, though."

She showed Lizzie the phone.

"We were eating lunch and I didn't see it. Are your mom and dad here?"

"They took the trailer to Austin to pick up a horse. I'm sorry I worried you. I didn't have anyone to pick me up at the hospital, so I called my parents. They wanted me to come home for the weekend, and since I didn't figure the bakery would open for a couple of days, I did."

She glanced around and saw the rest of us standing there. "Uh."

"We took a road trip," I said.

She smiled and nodded, but that smile did not reach her eyes. That was very un-Becky-like.

"Would y'all like some tea? Mom made me a batch before she left. And a giant pot of stew. They didn't know if they'd be back tonight and my mom's love language is food. It's a lot cooler in the house, come on."

"Sure," I said. "Tea sounds good."

The ranch house was made from Texas stone, which is the same sort of limestone my building is made out of. She took us through the back door and into the large, modern kitchen.

We settled in at the breakfast area with our tea. "I'm sorry you came all the way out here to check on me. I just had to get away—it still doesn't feel real. Do the police know who did it? And who was that guy? He's dead, isn't he? They tried to block me from seeing but there was a lot of blood on the floor."

She shivered. I'd done the same thing when I'd seen all that. She'd been gone since Friday, so she probably hadn't heard any of the gossip or read anything online. "The police don't know yet who killed him." I motioned toward Lizzie.

She sniffed and blinked several times. "He was someone I knew," she said. "He wasn't supposed to be in town until today. My guess is he saw you in there and thought it was me."

The pained terror on Becky's face said it all, as she tried to process the information. Lizzie hadn't mentioned who the victim was to Becky. Maybe she wanted to protect her privacy, though the truth would come out soon.

"I keep saying this but I'm so sorry, Lizzie," Becky cried. "I…should have done something. I don't know what. Everything is so hazy. I was bored Friday night, so I thought I'd get a head start for Saturday. I stayed later than I told you I would.

"I can't remember exactly what happened. I know amnesia is dumb. You see it in movies or in books and it seems unreal. But I swear, when I try to think about that night it's just darkness. When I woke up in the freezer, I thought Mrs. Whedon was dead, and I had a panic attack."

"It had to be very traumatic for you," Jasmine said. "Waking up like that. It's no wonder you can't remember every detail."

"She's right," Shannon added. "I've been in a similar situation with Ainsley, and it's so shocking that you can't wrap your head around it."

Becky rubbed her head. "Maybe I don't want to remember. I mean, I do. But the doctor told me that I might have seen something that scared me so bad I've pushed it away to protect myself. I couldn't stop shaking that night and it wasn't just from being in the freezer for so long. Mom had to put the electric blanket on me."

She'd probably been in shock. I could relate. I was surprised the hospital released her with a head injury and shock.

I nodded. "I don't want to force you to do anything, but my brother did an exercise for me and it helped me remember a few details. Do you mind if we try?"

Becky frowned and rubbed her head again.

Lizzie touched her shoulder. "You don't have to do anything that makes you feel uncomfortable," she said. "I'm just glad to know you're okay."

"No. I want to. He was your friend. We need to find out who…hurt him. I'll try. But honestly, I've been trying to remember and it's like that part of my brain is just gone."

"We'll just try it for a minute," I said. "You never know when the smallest detail might help."

"Okay," Becky said uneasily.

"Close your eyes and take a deep breath."

She did what I asked.

"Think about what you were doing right before your memory went blank."

"I locked the door after Lizzie left, or at least, I think I did. I shoved the keys in my pocket. Then I started gathering ingredients to make fruit kolaches. Lizzie likes to have everything ready first thing. I thought I might be able to sleep in a little if I did it the night before. I love working at the shop but it's so early every day. Not that I'm complaining."

She opened her eyes and stared at Lizzie.

"I know," she said. "Close your eyes."

"Okay, then what happened?" I asked gently.

"I couldn't remember if I'd made enough bread dough before I left. So, I opened the freezer door to see what we had on the slab. It looked like enough, but you can never be sure, especially on a Saturday morning. I decided to make some more so it could rise overnight. That way, Lizzie wouldn't have to stop everything to make dough. She works too hard."

Lizzie smiled at the girl and shook her head.

"I finished and was coming out of the freezer when I heard a noise. At first, I thought maybe I'd knocked something over inside, so I turned back around—and there's something. It's like right there on the edge of my mind." She raised her hand as if trying to grab a thought.

Then she screamed—and well, we all screamed, and a dog started barking.

Becky's eyes flashed open and tears streamed down her cheeks. "He said, 'I'm going to get you, girl,' and then his hands wrapped around me." She started sobbing.

We all shivered, and then Lizzie took the crying girl into her arms. "It's okay. You're safe," she whispered. The rest of us stared down at our tea. Poor Becky had been attacked. No wonder she couldn't remember anything.

I ran to find the bathroom so I could get her some tissues.

When I came back, she'd calmed down. I handed her the tissues so she could wipe her face.

"You were very brave," I said. "Are you okay?"

She nodded but didn't look terribly certain about that. "Everything goes black after that. I woke up with poor Mrs. Whedon in my arms. I'll be honest, I thought she was dead. My head hurt so bad and I felt sick. Kind of like I do now."

"You went through a lot," Shannon said. "Ainsley is right. You are so brave. I'd be way more of a mess than you are. Other than the bump on the head, did the doctors find anything else wrong with you?"

The young girl shook her head. "The bump wasn't that bad. I honestly don't remember going into the freezer but I was fine—other than being more scared than I ever had before."

"That makes sense," Shannon said. I understand why she'd asked that question. A man attacking a woman—I was just glad nothing else had happened. The poor thing had been through enough.

"Do you know when you'll open the bakery back up?" she asked.

"You don't worry about that, hon," Lizzie said. "And I understand if you need to quit. It's going to be tough for you to go back in there."

The stricken look on Becky's face surprised me. "No. I mean, I want to come back to work. It's the best job. I'm learning so much from you on how to bake and run a business. I know it won't be easy, but I'd like to stay."

"Of course, you can stay. I just didn't want you to feel like you had to work there. You've been through a lot."

"It's okay. We have a lot of good memories there. And the doctor said it might help me to remember more details, if I'm in familiar circumstances."

"Okay. If you're sure. I have to get things—uh—back in order. I thought maybe on Friday, if it's okay with the sheriff, we could get back to it."

Becky smiled. "That sounds good. I think I just need things to get back to normal."

"I promise we'll get out of your hair. But I have one more question for you."

Becky glanced at me warily. "Okay."

"Your friend next door mentioned a boyfriend. I was curious why you didn't call your boyfriend."

She stared at me strangely. "I don't have a boyfriend. I didn't even know anyone lived next door. I sometimes hear water running. I don't know why anyone would say that."

Some people liked to be part of the drama. I'd seen it before.

"Becky, your memories will come back," Jasmine said. "That happened for me. Don't stress about it and they'll come faster."

"She's right," I said. "Hang out with your horses and enjoy your day. Relax, and you never know what might happen."

I left out what was rolling around in my ear like an earworm.

It's okay, Becky, even if you are a killer.

Chapter Seven

A FEW DAYS later, I was working in the back of the shop when Lizzie stopped by with a box of something that smelled so good I wanted to eat the air.

"Hey, what's up?" I asked Lizzie.

"I brought you a treat."

I cringed. "I'm supposed to cut back on sugar." I started to hand the box back, but she waved it away.

"You and half the country. Lots of people need sugar-free treats, so I wondered if you could be my taste-tester for these chocolate chip cookies. No sugar, or gluten. Though, I can't be totally gluten-free in the shop because we use so much enriched flour. But try it."

I'm not a big fan of sugar-free anything, but I'd do just about anything for a friend.

I took a bite. The cookie was still warm, and the buttery, chocolate goodness melted in my mouth.

"Yum."

Lizzie clapped her hands. "Yay. I thought this batch tasted pretty good, but I wasn't sure. I've been working on them all afternoon."

"I can't tell they don't have sugar. They are just as good as your other ones."

"Awesome. I'm slowly going to add them into the regular

menu. Everyone deserves a treat. I, um, had another favor to ask you."

"What's that?"

"Will you go to Morton's funeral with me? Please? I know it's a lot to ask. Funerals pretty much suck. I just—I don't want to go alone. The truth is I need a buffer. If I'm alone, his mom'll pull the daggers out in front of her friends. But if I'm there with someone she's more likely to behave. Though, she should be grieving for her son, instead of picking on me."

I'd been trying to figure out a way to ask if she was going. The family was quite prominent in these parts, and there had been a long obit in the paper. After everything, it was weird seeing his face. Funerals were a great place to get some info about the deceased, and I needed it.

Mrs. Whedon still hadn't regained consciousness, and the police were low on suspects. That reminded me. Kane had never called me back.

I'd been curious if he figured out how tall the killer was and if that matched the person I'd seen in the park.

"I'd be happy to go with you. I'll even drive," I offered.

"Oh, that's sweet of you. I appreciate it. Like I told you, we had a long history. I really did love the guy and I'm going to miss him. I need this chance to say goodbye."

She blinked as if she were holding back tears.

I glanced down at the cookies. I'm terrible about crying when others cry these days. I never used to be that way. But now, even commercials get me sometimes.

"I'm going to close the bakery tomorrow, and the funeral is at eleven in Buda."

That was only about forty minutes away.

"I'll pick you up a little before ten. Is that okay?"

She nodded.

After she left, I called my friend Kane, who is the medical examiner. Greg had put the word out to keep me out of things but I had my ways. My call, like all the others lately, went straight to voice mail.

"You're avoiding me. But I know where to find you. Call me please. I just have one question. One. And I promise I won't bother you again."

"Today," I said as I hung up. I didn't like to make promises I couldn't keep.

LATER THAT EVENING, I had just let George out when my phone rang.

"Greg says I can't tell you anything—for real this time," Kane said before I could even answer hello. I chuckled.

"I won't tell if you don't."

He sighed. "What is it?"

"Do you have any idea how tall the assailant was?"

"What do you mean?" he asked.

"Those frying pans are heavy. I asked Lizzie about the one you guys have in evidence. It's one of the larger ones that can hold a lot of biscuits. She said she can barely lift it with two hands."

"Right. So, you're thinking it had to be someone tall and strong."

I shrugged, even though he couldn't see me. "You tell

me."

"That's one possibility. The lab reports on the clothing just came back. He had flour on his knees, so he must have hit the ground that way, but I'm having trouble with the physics of how he hit the table with that same side."

"Or if he'd stumbled and then fell," I said. "I mean, if he was lower, and then hit, his head may have swung and he hit the steel table that way."

My stomach twisted and bile rose in my throat. I put the can of soup I'd been about to heat up, back in the cabinet.

"The way the bone fragments were jammed in the brain, the two blows overlapped in a few places. Basically, the side of the head was smashed in."

Ugh.

"Can you tell the size of the assailant?"

"Why is this so important to you?"

"Did Greg tell you about the guy in the park?"

Kane cleared his throat. "I've been reading the reports."

"I was just curious if the killer could be that guy. I don't know anything about the victim, but I'm going with Lizzie to his funeral tomorrow. I thought, if I knew how tall the killer was—maybe I could keep an eye out."

There was silence.

"Did I lose you?" I asked.

"I'm going through my notes," Kane said. "The victim was five eleven—that just leaves too wide of a range to say for certain. Anyone his height or a little under, to a lot taller, could have done it. But they'd need to have good upper arm strength to swing that skillet as hard as they did."

"I've read about adrenaline and people in stressful situations. Could it be a woman?"

"I suppose. Like I said, though, I deal in facts and it's not something I can say conclusively."

"I'm looking for a man or woman five six or taller with good upper body strength."

Kane chuckled.

"Hey, we've started with less."

"True. The police don't have any leads either. I'm going through the reports now. They are looking into his family's business and his friends. But they haven't found anything."

"Thanks, Kane. I appreciate you telling me that. It saves me having to break into your office, or my brother's, to find out what's going on."

"You're a good detective, Ains. You have an eye for the personality aspect of an investigation. Just do us all a favor and be careful this time. Oh, that reminds me. Are you watching your blood sugar?" Between Kane, my brother, and Jake, it was like having three mother hens.

"Yes." I grabbed a piece of cheese from the fridge. I hadn't eaten much today. "Thanks for calling me back."

"Just don't tell your brother."

"No problem."

I hung up, and George went nuts outside. I turned on the back light, and then opened the door.

"George, stop that. Poor Mr. Squirrel has probably had enough." The squirrels and the woodland animals around here liked to play a game called "Let's Drive George Crazy." They were very good at it. My dog loved to play along most of the time. But every once in a while they'd intrude on what he considered his space inside the fence. Then all heck would break loose.

"George, come here." I used my stern voice.

My property backed up to a forest and there were teens out there in the summer hanging out at the lake that was about a mile from my property. There was a worn path through the woods that a lot of them used. Jake had found it when he'd been clearing the underbrush from around his place, which is about a mile in the other direction.

He was working the night shift this week, so we hadn't seen each other much.

George wouldn't stop barking and there were no woodland animals to be found.

"George. Now!" I didn't yell at him often. It hurt his feelings. But he was freaking me out. He backed up, but continued barking. I grabbed the bat that I kept just inside the back door.

I was a woman who lived in the country alone. More than once, a killer had used those woods to spy on me. And then there was that one time when Jake's stalker had come around.

I would never let anyone scare me out of my house, but I did take precautions.

"I don't know who is out there," I yelled, "but my brother, the sheriff, put cameras on the back of my house. I'd suggest moving along. I also don't know how much longer my dog will stay inside the fence. He's been known to jump it a few times."

My voice was way more powerful than I felt. I tightened my hand on the bat. George moved closer, and then sat on my feet. It was his way of protecting me. I grabbed his collar and backed into the house. He'd stopped barking, so whoever or whatever it was must have been gone.

"Probably just kids," I said to George and to myself. After putting the bat down, my hands shook as I locked the back door.

The pool of blood flashed through my brain.

Had I seen the killer? Was he back there now stalking my house?

I shivered.

"George, bonus for you. You get to sleep in my room tonight."

Chapter Eight

THE NEXT AFTERNOON, Lizzie and I pulled up in front a large Baptist church just outside of Buda. The parking lot was full, so I circled around and parked on the street where several others had done the same thing.

"Your ex must have been very popular," I said.

"He was a charmer, and his mother's favorite," Lizzie said as she met me at the hood of the car. "Even though they disagreed about everything, he could do no wrong. My guess is that these are mostly her friends. Though, like I said, he was a charming son-of-a-gun. Swept me right off of my feet. I was so under his spell that I didn't see what was right in front of my face."

I crooked my arm in hers and we headed into the church. We found a seat in a middle pew. I liked sitting toward the back so I could keep an eye on people, but I followed her lead.

The church filled up quickly. A few minutes later, the family filed in, sitting in the first two pews.

The service was formal and a couple of hymns were sung.

A man got up to speak. He was handsome in a ruffled kind of way. He shoved his curls out of his eyes and then sighed into the microphone.

"Sorry. This is hard," he said. "Mom wanted me to say a

few words about my brother. As you all know, he was a great guy. His family, friends, and employees loved him. He had a good heart and had a way of looking out for those in trouble. I think one of the best measures of a man is the reputation he leaves behind.

"My brother wasn't perfect, but being loved and missed by so many people here today shows us just what kind of man he was."

Another man wailed, across from of us, and then shoved a handkerchief in front of his face.

Everyone in the church stared at him. Poor guy. Was that his partner, perhaps? It would make sense.

The brother cleared his throat. "My brother always looked out for me," he said. "I was a terrible little guy. Mort would say a small demon who had the scream of a she-devil."

People laughed.

"But I learned how to treat people. I'll never have the patience he did nor the charm. But he taught me a lot about respecting others and myself." He choked up a bit, and my eyes watered.

"Mom and I would like to invite you to the house for a reception. All are welcome." He croaked the last words out and then ran off to sit by his mother.

A few other friends spoke. All of them said the same thing. He was a great guy. He was fun. And they all had funny anecdotes about him.

I felt like I knew Morton Gallagher by the time it was all over, and I'd never met the guy.

The family filed out, but they stopped at our pew.

"I know you killed my son," the mother said under her

breath to Lizzie. "I've already told the police everything. I expect you'll be arrested soon. We all know you never forgave him, even though it was *your* fault. I can't believe you had the nerve to show your face here."

Lizzie started to stand, but I grabbed her hand. His mother was grieving, but that did not give her the right to attack my friend.

I stood and faced the woman. "I'm truly sorry for your loss. I can't begin to understand what you, and your family, are going through. But you should know, ma'am, my friend was with witnesses when your son was killed. She wasn't there when he died. I beg of you to let her grieve her former husband and best friend—that's how she described him to me—in peace."

You can mess with me, but you don't mess with my friends.

The woman was about to open her mouth, but her son ushered her along. People around me were whispering and poor Lizzie's head was bowed and she pressed tissues to her face.

I hadn't meant to upset anyone. I had to do something about this serious case of foot-in-mouth disease I had. I'd just raised my voice to a grieving mother.

"Lizzie, I'm so sorry. I didn't mean to upset you." I put a hand on her shoulder. People around us were still whispering and I'm sure my cheeks had turned red.

Lizzie lifted her head, but she wasn't crying.

She giggled. "Mort would have loved that. He was the only one who could stand up to her. I swear that's why she loved him so much."

I took a deep breath. "My temper got the best of me and I didn't want people spreading rumors about you."

She smiled. "Ainsley, no one has ever taken up for me like that. I'm grateful to you."

"About time someone stood up to the old bat," a man's voice said from behind me.

I turned to find the man who had cried out during the service standing there. He was tall and lanky, and wore a very expensive suit.

He held out a hand. "I'm Jerome. I was Mort's assistant and his friend," he whispered that last word.

I shook his hand. "I'm Ainsley, and I'm sorry for your loss."

"I'm guessing you are Lizzie?" he asked my friend.

She nodded and shook his hand.

"He talked about you a lot," he said. "I'm pretty sure you were the platonic love of his life."

Lizzie stood. "Oh, are you Jere? He adored you." She reached her arms out and hugged him across me.

"Thanks. Best boss and friend I ever had. A bunch of us, his real friends, are getting together later. The Mexican restaurant is just up the road. Would you like to join us?"

I had a feeling our invitation to the family gathering was no longer valid.

"Ainsley was sweet enough to bring me and I don't want to keep her."

"It's okay." I was still sitting down, and they were so close, I couldn't quite get up. I awkwardly slid down the pew and freed myself. "I'm sure you'd love to meet his friends."

"Are you sure?" She turned to face me.

I nodded. My phone buzzed. It was Shannon.

"I'll meet you outside. I need to take this."

I headed out into the fresh air. It was hot, but the church had been freezing. It would take a minute for me to defrost.

"Tell me everything," Shannon said.

I laughed. "The funeral just ended," I whispered. There were still people milling around.

"Any suspects yet?"

"Nope. Everyone loves him. Or loved him. We met his assistant and we're going to a gathering to meet more of his friends. Other than the mother was nasty to poor Lizzie in front of everyone, I don't have anything to report."

"Okay, but I want a full rundown tonight. Oh, and Jasmine wants to know if we can reschedule girls' night for Friday, since the last one was—uh—interrupted."

That was one way of putting it. "Sure. Jake's on nights. I'll check with Lizzie and get back to you."

I was about to go back inside, when a woman stopped me. She was very sophisticated in a green dress, and black heels. She reminded me of Oprah in a way.

"I'm sorry to bother you, but I was curious if the woman sitting with you was Elizabeth Hernandez."

I wasn't sure what to say. "Uh, may I ask who you are?"

She smiled, as if to put me at ease about any stranger danger. "I apologize, I should have introduced myself. And good for you for being protective of your friend. I'm Latonda Price, the estate lawyer for Mr. Gallagher. I needed to speak with her about a private matter considering the deceased."

She was so formal, I believed her.

"Yes, that's Lizzie."

Lizzie and Jere walked out of the vestibule.

"Thank you," she said.

I followed her over.

"Oh, good. You're both here. Elizabeth Hernandez and Jerome Clark, correct?"

"Yes," Jere said warily.

The lawyer explained who she was. "I realize this is terrible timing and that you are grieving, but I have instructions to speak with you before I have any dealings with the family. They've been asking about his will, and I'd appreciate if we could speak now. At least, before you attend the reception."

Jere and Lizzie stared at one another and then back at the lawyer.

"I—I don't think I'm invited to the reception," Lizzie said carefully.

"Me either," said Jere. "I'll be lucky if I have a job on Monday. Mrs. Gallagher never liked me. Mainly because I'd screen her calls for Mort."

"I see. Would it be possible for you to come to the office? I promise it will only take a half hour or so. Mr. Gallagher made provisions for you both in his will."

They stared at each other again, and then back at her. "Provisions?" Jere asked.

"Yes. I'll need you to sign some papers and we'll need a witness." She glanced at me.

"What time is the gathering?" Lizzie asked Jere.

"Not for a couple of hours. We have time."

The woman handed business cards to Lizzie and Jere.

"If you could meet me there in ten minutes, we'll go through everything. Again, a half hour to forty-five minutes at the most."

"I CAN'T IMAGINE what this is all about," Lizzie said, as we pulled up in front of a new office building. "Everything should go to his family. Maybe there's something from his house he wanted me to have. He and I both love art. This day is weird. I'm so glad you're here."

"Me, too."

"You are such a blessing Ainsley. None of this feels real. I can't explain it." She wrung her hands again and her voice shook when she spoke.

"I get it. I promise and I will always be here for you."

The office was on the third floor, and it was grand, as in sparkling new and almost space-age-looking the way the offices were set up.

The receptionist started to speak, but the lawyer motioned for us to follow her.

Jere and Lizzie took the chairs in front of her desk, and I sat on a leather sofa behind them.

"As I said, Mr. Gallagher insisted I speak with you as soon as possible after his death. I would have contacted you sooner, but I was in Dallas on another case."

"It's okay," Lizzie said.

"I'm dying to know what this all about," Jere said.

So was I, though I would never admit it.

"Should I leave for this part?" I asked.

Lizzie shook her head. "Please stay. I'm worried I'm going to miss something," she said. "I do that at the doctor, like I know I should be paying attention, but then I miss the most important part."

"I got you," I said. "Jere, is that okay with you?"

He shrugged. "I'm the same as Lizzie. Just pay attention for us."

The lawyer laughed. "I hope I'm not that boring." She lifted a huge pile of papers onto the desk.

"This paperwork looks scary, but it's straightforward," the attorney continued.

"What is that?" Jere asked.

"Mr. Gallagher has given you equal shares of the company. Between the two of you, you'll have fifty-one percent ownership. And he's made provisions for you both to sit on the board of directors."

"What?" Lizzie's voice was strangled. "I don't want anything to do with those people."

"I don't understand," Jere said.

"May I speak frankly?" The lawyer leaned forward and put her elbows on her desk.

"Yes," Jere said.

"I had several long conversations with Mr. Gallagher about his wishes. He trusted you two with the future of the company. He did not expect you to work there full-time, just when the board of directors meet. He feared his brother, who gets fifty percent of the shares, would not be able to stand up to their mother, who he believed, did not always have the best interests of the company or its employees in mind when making financial decisions.

"Ms. Hernandez, he asked that you be reminded about your idea to take the company organic seven years ago and your plan for how they could do that by subsidizing the farmers. He said it's the main reason the company jumped ahead of competitors years ago.

"And, Mr. Clark, he told me you've been a faithful friend, and that he had tried to move you into management several times, but you refused. He said to trust yourself and your ideas, as they are always thoughtful and excellent."

Jere sniffled.

"I believe he says about the same in your letters." She handed them each an envelope. "He trusted the two of you would work together to move the company forward. In fact, he stated in the documents to his family, that there were no two people he trusted more."

Lizzie glanced down at her hands. I couldn't see her face, but I grabbed two small packages of tissues from my purse, and handed one to each of them.

I didn't know his family but I had a feeling they were not going to be happy when they found out about all of this, especially his mother.

"Darn him," Lizzie croaked, and then she laughed, somewhat hysterically.

Then Jere started laughing. They howled and held on to each other.

The attorney glanced at me and I shrugged my shoulders. Then, we both smiled.

I have that same problem with inappropriate laughing. I'm just glad I didn't do it during the funeral.

The pair finally pulled themselves together.

"Whew, sorry about that," Jere said. "You probably think we're nuts."

"Not at all," the lawyer said.

"We are. Do you understand what he's asking us to do? This is the big finger to his mom. He loved her, but he also thought she was the devil incarnate. I take it they don't know anything about this."

"No," the attorney said. "Though his brother and mother have both reached out. There is a meeting set at the end of the week. I needed time to speak to the both of you first. This is a great deal of information for you to take in, and it was important that you hear the news as quickly as possible."

"Trust me, we understand," Lizzie said. "I also appreciate that you did not invite us to hear all of this together. They probably would have killed us before we got out the door."

Was that the reason Mort had been murdered? Maybe, one of the family members found out about the will. Finally, we had a lead. Money is a big motive for murder. People are greedy.

"It's not my place, but did he make changes to his will recently?" I asked.

"We went over it in the last six months on the phone. I do that with all of my clients. But this will hasn't changed for three years."

"Oh, wow," Jere said.

"This wasn't some *mom made me mad this week* decision," Lizzie added. "He wanted us to do this."

"Man, I had no idea." Jere's voice was hoarse, as if he were trying not to cry. "There were some tough times a year ago with his family trying to get him kicked off the board of directors. I promised I would die for him, but he was not allowed to give up. Luckily, he owned the controlling interest. And the courts saw it that way," Jere said. "If he hadn't, so many farmers would have been put out of business because of the way things were set up. Mort said it was more important to invest in the people who provide the product."

"Do you think he maybe wondered if they'd try to kill him to get control?" I asked. And then threw my hand over my mouth. "Sorry. None of my business."

Lizzie shook her head. "His mother loved him a little too much. I can't imagine her trying to hurt him."

Jere frowned. "You haven't been around them the last few years. She was not happy with the golden boy. They would have made millions by being publicly traded, and all that woman has ever really loved is money."

Wow. Like I thought, money and greed. The two top reasons people were murdered.

I needed to call my brother.

Chapter Nine

WHEN I FINALLY arrived home, all I wanted was a nap. But Jake's truck was in my driveway. I'd really missed him the last few days. It's funny how fast you can get used to someone always being around.

I was about to yell, "Honey, I'm home," when I stepped in, but a snore stopped me. Jake and George were on the couch sound asleep. My boyfriend must have worn my dog out for him to sleep so hard he didn't hear me coming into the house.

As I tiptoed past them, George lifted his head and opened one sleepy eye. Then he grunted and lay back down.

Yep. They definitely did something to wear them both out.

I put my stuff on the kitchen bar. The oven was on, so I checked the timer. It still had a half hour to go. It looked like lasagna. I loved Jake's cooking, but I was surprised he'd make a lasagna because of the sugar in the sauce. Maybe he was making it for the guys at the station but he'd better give me a piece.

I had every intention of changing clothes and then going back downstairs, but my bed looked so inviting.

The next thing I knew, I had drool on the corner of my mouth and there were voices downstairs. Jake must have been talking to George.

I yawned. I'd only been asleep a half hour, but I had that drugged zombie feeling. I washed my face and changed into comfy clothes, which was one of my giant unicorn T-shirts and the oldest pair of jean shorts I owned. They were so bad that I only wore them around the house.

But when I turned the corner downstairs, I almost ran right back up.

My dining table was full of people.

"Uh."

Jake walked in with a salad, and kissed me on the cheek.

"Gang's here for dinner," he said.

"Kane just texted that he'll be here in five," my brother said. Lucy, a detective who worked with him and lived in his house—but they swore they weren't dating—sat next to him. Shannon and Mike were also there, as was Jasmine.

Our little gang had grown. "Hi. I didn't know we were having company," I said. "Do you need help?" I asked Jake.

"Nope. Everything is ready. Go ahead and sit down."

My brain was still in zombie mode and I wasn't really in the mood to be social. But I loved all these people, so I sat my butt down.

"Greg was at the coffee shop and said he'd be stopping by tonight to catch up," Shannon said. "And you probably don't remember—I know Jake and Mike forgot—that we were having dinner tonight." She smiled weirdly. "I mean, that was before the funeral and stuff. But I figured, we all had to eat. And then Greg said Kane was also coming, so I invited Jasmine."

Jasmine smiled knowingly.

Oh. Ohhh. Right. This was Shannon's idea. I had a feeling everyone knew exactly what was going on. My friend was not going to be left out of this conversation with my brother.

"I—did remember—yesterday," I said, covering for my friend. "But it was quite the day and I crashed as soon as I came home."

"Funerals always wear me out," Jasmine said.

Then it was really quiet as Jake brought in the lasagna. Funny, since this crowd was usually so loud we'd been asked to tone it down a few times when in restaurants.

I give my brother a hard time but he isn't dumb. He glanced around the table and then smirked. "Just tell us what happened," Greg said. "But wait for Kane, or he'll feel left out."

Everyone laughed. Kane walked in—none of them ever knocked anymore—and went to the bathroom to wash his hands. Then he sat down by Jasmine. They'd gone on a few dates, but she was still dealing with a lot of family stuff so they were taking things slow.

"Spill," Shannon said.

I told them everything. From the mean mom, to the fact our friend Lizzie was in the middle of a crazy family feud.

"Did anyone fit your description?" Kane asked, and then stuck a forkful of lasagna in his mouth.

"What description?" Greg asked.

Kane's eyes opened wider. "I called Kane a while back to ask if him if he could tell the height of the person who killed Mort, but he said it was too big of a range. I've been wondering all this time if that guy I saw in the park had something to do with it. But Kane, reluctantly mentioned that the person would have a lot of arm strength to swing—well, uh, so hard." We were eating dinner. There was no reason to go over those details.

"And?"

I shrugged. "Only most of the people at the church." As I said it, a vision of the back of a man's neck came into my mind but he wasn't from the church.

I closed my eyes. It was the guy from the park. When he ran past, there was something on his neck. The top of an I or an L, with a fancy serif. And then it was gone.

When I opened my eyes, everyone was staring at me.

"What did you see?" Lucy asked. She had her pen and notebook. I don't know where she kept them, but they always seemed to be in her hand.

"It won't help," I said. "I can only see the top of it."

"Just tell us," Greg said.

"It was either the letter L or I on his neck. The T-shirt he wore covered the rest. But it was words tattooed, or a mark. I only saw it for a second as his arm came down when he was running. And it was so dark, it could have been a shadow."

Greg rubbed the bridge of his nose. He always did that when he was thinking hard about something. "When did you say the reading of the will is?"

"The lawyer said at the end of the week. I'm worried Gran and Becky might be in danger. You say the killer is probably far away, but what if someone found out about the will?"

My brother frowned and stared down at his plate. He hated when I was right.

"Ainsley may be onto something," Lucy said. "With that

much money on the line, we're going to need more staff. We've got to cover the hospital, the baker, her assistant and your sister."

Jake's fork clattered to the plate. "Why is Ains in danger?"

"She may have seen the killer and the family knows her face. My guess is they would hire someone, which might make it easier."

Wait. A hired killer. I wasn't so hungry anymore. Mrs. Whedon and Becky might have seen him, as well.

"Maybe they had him follow the victim and wanted him to make it look like the baker had done it. But the family, from what Ainsley says, wasn't that close anymore. They might not know they were still such good friends. Setting her up backfired. We better cover all the bases on Friday. Maybe, before. She's right—maybe they already know. They could have been after the baker and were surprised by the victim."

"Yeah," Greg grumbled. "Better let the team know. Ains, is there anything else?"

I still wasn't awake yet. Maybe, I should have had some coffee before this conversation. "You're worried about people in the crosshairs, right?"

He nodded. "You better protect Jere—he was Mort's assistant. Half of those shares go to him."

"I'll contact the chief of police over there. They need to watch the house anyway."

The house. "Oh, one more thing. The house, and the ranch they live on, all belongs to Lizzie now. After a few tequila shots at our late lunch, she was ready to go over there and kick them out. Luckily, she passed out in my car before she could follow through. She's at home sleeping it off."

Greg rubbed his head again. "Do you think she'll do it?"

I shook my head. "I don't think she'll go anywhere near them sober. But it's one more reason for them to be angry with her."

"We can't cover all of them," Lucy said. "Not in the middle of tourists season. And then we have the festival next week."

Crud. The festival. With all the drama, I'd forgotten about it. I needed to check and make sure our booth was ready to roll. And I still hadn't gone over the sketches for the float.

"And it's Ainsley's birthday," Shannon added.

"If it will help, they could stay with me this weekend," Jasmine said. "I have a security team with me at all times and we were already doing a girls' weekend for Ainsley's birthday."

"That's very sweet of you," I said, "but I have to work. At least, part of Saturday. And Lizzie won't want to close the bakery again. Or maybe she will. I know she's dealing with too much right now."

"Are you sure?" Greg asked Jasmine, as if I weren't sitting right here.

"Yes. You guys have all done so much for me. I'm happy to help out. That way, at least on Friday, they are all in one place, except for Mrs. Whedon."

"Jasmine, I can have them come here," I said. "I don't want to put you out."

"My house is bigger. I don't mean that as a brag, but until this case is cleared up, it will be easier for everyone. If

Lizzie wants to work, one of my guys can take her into the bakery, and then maybe Greg's guys can keep an eye out. It's just for the weekend, and it'll be fun. Besides, if you stay here, you'll just sit around and worry."

I was going to worry no matter what. I glanced at the back door. What if the killer had been out in the woods behind my house?

"Okay. I'll see what I can do about shifts at the store. But I've been missing a lot."

Shannon shook her head. "Everyone loves you, and all you have to do is tell them to be on the lookout for a killer with a tattoo on his neck."

"No!" Greg shouted.

Shannon and I jumped.

"Sorry," he said. "It's just, the fewer people who know about all of this, the better. And the last thing we want is the killer to know we're closing in."

"All right." Shannon frowned. "But if I see someone walk into the shop with a tattoo on their neck, I'm calling you."

Greg rolled his eyes.

"I've got to work on Friday night, but I can help keep an eye out on Saturday," Jake said.

"Me too," Kane added.

Jasmine stared at him.

"What?"

"It's a girls' weekend and I have security guards."

"Right, so two more won't hurt," he said. "We'll stay out of your way. It's a big house."

I laughed and covered it with a cough.

He reminded me of Jake when he was in protective mode.

"Wait. I thought you had to work tonight?" I turned to Jake.

He grinned. "What? And miss out on all of this? That's why I have to work Friday. I traded with one of the guys."

I felt like we had our own little Scooby gang. We even had the Great Dane. Well, right now George was passed out on the sofa in his favorite spot.

"Then it's settled," said Greg. "We'll see what happens after the reading of the will. Ainsley, when you went to lunch, did you meet anyone who might have been a former lover? Anyone who might fit that bill?"

I chewed on my lip, and I tried to remember who was at the big table where we'd eaten. I'd been more focused on the fact that Jere and Lizzie were going shot-for-shot with the tequila.

"No. But I could ask Jere. He was also Mort's friend. He might know. I can call to check up on him. He was pretty rough when I dropped him off at his apartment."

"I want everyone at this table to understand something. We are looking at the family, but this also could have been a jealous lover. Or a robbery interrupted. We have absolutely no proof the family had anything to do with the murder or that they know about the will. Do you understand? The killer could be anyone," Greg lectured. "Be aware of your surroundings at all times.

"This is not a game." He stared at me when he said that. "Anyone who might have seen the killer is in danger. Don't go anywhere alone and make sure someone knows your whereabouts at all times."

"That's a weird word."

Greg frowned at me.

"Whereabouts. It's two words put together that have just never made sense to me. I just always thought it was weird."

Everyone around the table chuckled.

Greg sighed. "Ains, promise me you'll be careful."

"I will." It's not like I tried to get into trouble. For some reason, it always seemed to find me.

Chapter Ten

THE NEXT MORNING, Jake dropped George and me off at the shop. I put my stuff in the office and went through the store before anyone else arrived.

Sometimes I forgot all of this was mine. It was such a team effort with all my artists and craftspeople. I was living the dream and I worked with some of the most amazing humans I'd ever met.

I walked by Mrs. Whedon's booth. All of her beautiful yarn was stacked neatly. Jake had promised to pick me up at lunch to go visit her at the hospital. They'd moved her out of ICU, so at least there was that.

I straightened up her stacks the way she liked them, and then went back to get some inventory. By the time I'd finished cleaning up her booth, several of the other vendors had arrived.

We all worked in sync getting ready to open the shop. I never had to tell anyone what to do. They just did it. I'd never worked anywhere like my shop Bless Your Art. It's true what they say. Surround yourself with the best people and you'll be amazed by the results.

It was like walking into my happy place every day. Though, sometimes, especially during the busy seasons, I had to remind myself that I was living my dream.

Around lunchtime, things slowed down a bit. As promised, Jake showed up. Carrie promised to take George for his afternoon stroll, so I headed out.

When we arrived at the hospital, Jake pulled two lunch bags out of the back seat of his truck. "I thought we could have lunch with Gran."

I kissed his cheek. "You are the best man ever."

He laughed. "I try. I know it's tough for you. She's family, but I feel like the more normal we pretend things are, the more likely she is to come back to us."

I nodded. There was no way I could speak, I was so choked up. I was in love with a man, who was so thoughtful. A guy who would sit in a hospital room with his girlfriend and eat a sack lunch to keep Gran company.

I guess it's a day for remembering blessings.

A bit of her color had come back to her face, and several of the tubes had been taken out. The nurse was checking her vitals when we walked in.

"How is she?" Jake asked.

"Doc says pretty good. The swelling has gone down a great deal in the last forty-eight hours. And we've seen more REM activity in the eyes. That's usually a great sign."

My heart flipped in my chest with joy.

"Is she out of danger?" I asked.

"Medical professionals will never say for sure, but that she's improving at a steady rate is great. Her blood pressure, which was going from extreme highs to lows, has settled down."

After she left, I sat down. I was on one side of the bed, Jake on the other.

"Hey, Gran, Jake and I decided to have lunch with you today."

"That's right, Gran," Jake said. "I have to make Ains's lunch now so that I know she'll eat something besides cookies all day."

"Ya pass out from blood sugar problems one time, and the man goes crazy. I'm not going to lie though, his lunches are really good."

I opened my first plastic container. "Whoo-hoo, hummus. Gran, you know how much you love Jake's hummus. If you wake up, I'll share. And yes, that's a bribe."

We sat and ate in silence for a bit. After I finished, I went to take her hand, and noticed bruising.

"Jake, look at this."

I showed him and he frowned. "Was that there before?"

"You don't think someone here hurt her, do you?" My blood boiled. Anyone who hurt an old woman while she was in a coma was lower than rot.

He shook his head. "No. Don't get upset, Ains. The bruising could have happened when she was attacked and is just now showing up. She's pretty tan from working in her garden, and it could be it was there but none of us noticed."

I took a deep breath. "I'm calling Kane."

Of course, he didn't answer. It wasn't my fault he outed himself the night before. He was the one who brought up the height thing.

"Stop screening my calls. I'm in Mrs. Whedon's room and there's something…I need you to look at her hands. Please, Kane. Come as fast as you can."

My stomach swirled and acid came up my throat. I

would make sure she was never alone again. Even if this had happened during the scuffle.

My phone dinged. *Heading that way*, Kane texted.

A few minutes later, he texted for the room number and I gave it to him.

He came in with his doctor bag. That's where he kept a lot of his CSI stuff.

"What is it?"

Jake explained what we'd seen.

Kane took out a big scope-like thing, with a big light, and gently put her hand on the table that went over her bed.

He studied her hand for what seemed like forever. Then he put the scope away.

"Did someone hurt her?"

He shook his head. "I don't think so. These are several days old."

He bent her fingers and then looked at the bruising again.

"It isn't possible. No." He was talking to himself. Then he took the scope out and looked again. "I need to get back to my office to look at something."

He grabbed his bag and headed for the door.

"Kane. Stop. Please. Tell me what's going on."

"It looks like she punched someone," he said. "I examined her from head to toe the other night. Her hands were red, because of her body temperature. But I didn't notice any bruising then. But those are a few days old. She hit someone. Maybe our victim. That's what I have to take a look at."

Had Gran seen someone attacking Becky and punched them? I wouldn't have put it past her. She was a tough one, and strong for a woman her age.

My eyes went wide. I stared at Gran and then back at Kane.

This time I was the one shaking my head. "No. It isn't possible."

"What?" Jake asked.

"That Gran is the killer. Or at least, had some part in whatever happened. But then how did she end up injured in the freezer? She didn't throw herself in there and hit her head on the slab."

"I can't see her lifting up that skillet," Kane said. "Let alone, swinging it. She has a tiny frame."

"I've known Gran a long time," Jake said. "She never ceases to surprise me. If she thought she was saving Becky's life, there's no telling what she might have done."

He wasn't wrong. She'd lived a rather interesting life.

My hands were in fists and I forced them to relax. "None of it makes sense though. She landed on top of Becky in the freezer. Someone had to have pushed her in there." My mind whirled with a thousand possibilities at once.

"What were you going back to your office to look at?" I asked. My mind was so cluttered, I couldn't remember if he told me.

"The victim had contusions on the side of his face that wasn't smashed in and we weren't sure what caused them. Those contusions may match her knuckles. I need to get back to look at the photos."

"Maybe she hit him because she mistook him for a robber or thought he was trying to hurt Becky. But then—what? He tosses her in the freezer and someone else comes in and kills him?"

As I said it, things began to click in my head. There was a good chance Gran and Becky believed Mort was an intruder. Maybe he heard the killer coming and shoved them in the freezer.

"Why does she look like that?" Kane asked. "Is she in a trance?"

"She just figured something out," Jake answered.

Or. He heard Mrs. Whedon coming and then shoved Becky in the freezer. Then Mrs. Whedon hit him with a frying pan—and killed him.

"I have a theory. I'm not ready to share," I said. "Can you be a hundred percent certain that she hit him?"

Kane shrugged. "Ainsley, I'm pretty good at my job. I'd say I'm about eighty percent sure right now before I even look at the photos. I spent a lot of time trying to figure out what had caused that bruising. Most of the time when someone receives a punch, you can see indention a bit better. But she's older, so she probably didn't hit him that hard."

"Right. So she hit him, but there is no way to prove she killed him. And that she ended up in the freezer, as well, means she couldn't have dealt the death blow."

"My brain hurts," Jake said.

"Mine too," Kane added.

"It's a working theory. I'll put it in my report but I won't send it to your brother just yet. I need to do some more tests."

"Kane, how much does that pan weigh?"

"It's a big one, about twelve pounds. But it would take one heck of a swing to do damage like that. She's in her eighties and maybe weighs a hundred pounds."

Kane pressed his lips together. "You're right. So what are you thinking?"

"The victim may have shoved them in the freezer to save their lives. If someone was after him, that might have been what he wanted to tell Lizzie. It would explain why he came to town two days earlier than expected. Given the contents of his will, he might have been worried about her safety."

"It makes sense," Jake said. "From what you said last night people genuinely liked him, maybe even more than they did the rest of the family. If the killer was chasing him, maybe he just did what he could to save the others."

"Or he was getting them out of the way so he could fight," Kane added. "There were scratches on his arms, but those were from Becky. His DNA was under her nails. Like I said, I'm not one for assumptions. But you may be on the right track. I'll call you after I have a chance to do a bit more work on this."

He left, and I sat back down in the chair.

"Gran, I need you to wake up right now and tell me what happened. This is driving me crazy."

But she didn't answer and the ominous silence didn't help. What if the killer came back for her?

Wait. The guard who had been posted outside her door hadn't been there.

I jumped up and flung open the door.

No one was there.

"What is it?" Jake asked.

"We have a problem."

Chapter Eleven

Jake and I waited in Mrs. Whedon's room until my brother showed up. I wanted to yell and scream but I had a sneaking suspicion it wasn't his fault.

Jake pulled me into his arms, probably to stop my pacing. I did that when I was worried. "Maybe it was some kind of mix-up," he offered.

I shook my head. "Greg was just as surprised as I was that no one was outside the door of Gran's room." He'd promised last night that he'd keep it covered.

"Someone could have come in here and—"

"But they didn't," Jake said. "She's fine and her vitals are great. I've been watching them since I came in."

He squeezed me tight. I wrapped my arms around his waist and soaked up the strength he was giving me. "Take a deep breath, hon. We'll make sure she's protected."

"I don't know what I'd do without you."

"You're never going to have to find out."

I called the shop to tell them I'd be late, and Mike answered. I explained why I wasn't back yet.

"You stay there," he said. "I promise you by the end of today, you won't have to worry about her ever being alone. We had that going for the first few days, but everyone has been so busy getting ready for the festival. But she's our priority now. One of us will always be there. We protect our family."

I had to blink back tears. The people who showed their wares in my shop were so much more than coworkers, they really had become family.

"Thank you."

Not long after that, Greg walked in with his angry face. I prayed it wasn't directed at me.

"There won't be a problem from now on," he bit out. "Kevin was stationed outside the room but says a blond woman said she'd sit with Gran for a bit and that he should take a break."

He nearly growled his words. If I wasn't so mad at him, I might have felt sorry for Kevin. "Did you check the security cameras?" Jake asked.

"That's my next stop. The nurses say they didn't see her."

"Maybe the tapes will show something," Jake said. "I'll stay here. Why don't you and Ainsley go take a look."

My brother opened his mouth to disagree, but I held up a hand. "I'm going."

He nodded. "Jake, I've got Clyde coming in for the first watch. He should be here in a quarter hour."

"Okay. Go, you two." He shooshed us out the door.

"I know you're mad at me," Greg said as we moved quickly down the hallway. I had no idea where we were going but the hospital wasn't that big. It only had two floors.

"I'm not," I said. "I'm scared for her. If we hadn't shown up when we did—I don't even want to think about what might have happened."

At the end of the hall, he knocked on the door that said *security*. A heavy-set man in a blue uniform opened the door.

"Sheriff."

"Hey Ronny. This is my sister Ainsley. She's—helping with the investigation. Did you take a look?"

The other man nodded. "I've got it ready for you."

They only had cameras in the long hallways.

The first part of the video showed Kevin sitting just outside the door reading a comic book. A little bit later, a woman with a hat showed up and talked to Kevin. She wore a floral dress and high heels. There was something familiar about her.

The young deputy left, and the woman stood there for a minute. Then she glanced down the hall both ways, and pushed open the hospital room door.

The woman went in for about five minutes, and then came back out and had a tissue in her hand.

The nurse we'd seen in the room when we came in passed the woman in the hall, but she'd been staring down at her charts. The nurse entered the room without ever looking up.

Then Jake and I came into view.

"Uh," I said.

My healthy lunch did a turn in my stomach. Even though her face wasn't visible, she was familiar. I just couldn't place her.

"We should move the patient to the second floor," Ronny said. "I can code the elevator so that only one of our guys can punch it in for visitors. And we'll lock the side entrances."

"Ronny, are you sure you don't want to come work for me?" Greg asked.

The man chuckled. "I'd never pass the health exam."

Greg patted him on the shoulder.

"The other thing is that she doesn't lift her head once. It's like she knows those cameras are there," Ronny said. "With that hat on, there's no way to identify her, unless someone on the staff got a good look. Did your guy have a description?"

Greg grunted. "No. Other than she was taller than him, which we can see here, and she was older. He said maybe in her late fifties or early sixties. She had that plastic kind of face."

"Like she had too much plastic surgery?" I asked.

"Yes," Greg answered.

The body shape seemed familiar. She was tall and extra curvy.

"Excuse me, Ronny. Can you back that up to right before she opens the door?"

He rewound it and then paused the tape.

The diamonds on her hand. Every finger was covered with large rings.

I closed my eyes. Where had I seen those?

"Funeral," I said out loud. "Oh. No. That's her."

"Who?" Greg asked.

"You're not going to believe this, and I only saw her once for a short time, but she made an impression. I'm fairly certain that's Mrs. Gallagher, Mort's mom."

"What?" Greg coughed. I patted him on the back.

"Maybe if we see her vehicle, we can confirm it's her."

Ronny shook his head. "Sorry. We have them out the front but not in the parking areas. It's a small town and we have a pretty small budget for security."

"I understand," I said. "I'm grateful for your help." If only she'd looked up.

"What if she goes to Lizzie? She might know the truth."

Greg and I looked at each other.

"The bakery." We said it at the same time.

He took off running so fast, there was no way I could keep up with him.

I slid to a stop in front of Gran's room. I already couldn't breathe. Running is something I just didn't do.

Jake jumped up. "Is everything okay? Did you see who it was?"

I struggled for breath. "Greg's gone to the bakery to check on Becky and Lizzie. We think—" I gasped for breath. "What if she tries to hurt them?"

As much as I wanted to run after my brother, I would not leave Gran alone. "Will you go? Please? Make sure they are all right?"

I closed my eyes. They would be fine. They would be fine. They would be fine.

"I'm not leaving you, Ainsley. Greg has it handled. But you're in just as much danger."

There was a knock on the door, and I might have screamed. In my defense, I was a bit on edge.

The door slammed open, and Deputy Clyde was there with his gun. "Police," he said sharply.

"Sorry, Clyde. You scared me." My hands were shaking so hard that Jake took them in his.

"Ains had a bit of an upset," Jake said.

Clyde nodded as if that explained everything.

"You there?" Greg's voice crackled through Clyde's walkie-talkie.

"Yeah, boss."

"Tell my sister the bakery is secure."

I nodded.

"She heard you."

The knot in my stomach released.

"You two can go on if you want," Clyde said. "I have instructions to move Mrs. Whedon upstairs. The staff is getting her room ready now."

"Okay. But just so you and the other officers know, family and friends will be doing shifts by her bedside. We want to make sure—uh…"

"That she has someone close when she wakes up," Jake finished for me. "We'll make sure you have a list of names."

"All right. They'll need to bring IDs. We'll be checking those closely from here on out."

I forced myself to smile. "Thank you."

His walkie-talking crackled. "Get my sister to the station ASAP."

What now?

Chapter Twelve

JAKE CAME INSIDE the station with me. Kevin was at the front desk with his head hung low. My brother was fair, but he expected excellence from his deputy. As much as I wanted to feel sorry for him, he'd put Gran's life in danger.

Not that I thought Mort's mom would kill her.

Or would she? If she'd found out about the will, and that she had lost her home… People had murdered for less.

I headed back to Greg's office. He was in there grabbing some photos.

"What's up?" Jake asked.

"We pulled her over for a broken taillight and she assaulted the deputy."

Oh. My. That woman was unreal.

"She also doesn't have a license. She's already lawyered up, but I was wondering if you could do that thing you do?"

I pursed my lips. "What do you mean?"

"Where you get people to talk to you casually."

My eyes went wide, and Jake chuckled behind me.

"Gregory McGregor, are you asking me to help? And to spy on that woman?"

He sighed wearily. "Yes."

"Get me a cup of tea and a cup of coffee."

After he did what I asked, I carried them to the interview

room. "Greg, are you in here?" Then I stopped short when I saw her.

"Mrs. Gallagher? Are you okay?"

She narrowed her eyes at me. "Do I know you?"

Thank goodness she didn't remember. "No, ma'am, but I was, uh, friends with Mort. He was just the sweetest."

Her lip trembled and a tear fell to her cheek. "I miss him so much. That boy could get in my craw, but I just loved him to death. I can't believe he's gone. A parent should not outlive their child. I don't know what I'm going to do."

"Um. I'm so very sorry for your loss. Let me find you some tissues. This is coffee, and that's tea." I sat the cups on the table. "Take one if you need one or I can get you a bottle of water."

"Can you bring some cream and sugar for the coffee?"

"Of course. I'll be right back."

The coffee bar at the station was in the back. I ran to get everything and came back.

"Here you go." I handed her an entire box of tissues.

"Did something else happen? It's not like you haven't been through enough already." I gave her my sad face.

She dabbed her nose. "I lost my temper and they hauled me in like a common criminal. I was upset. My son was killed in this awful town. My detective that we keep on staff is useless. But he did find out others had been hurt that night. One of them was some old woman. Of course, he left out the fact that she's in a coma. He won't have a job when I get home." She waved the tissue. "Especially after all of this."

Rude.

"You'd think they'd understand I'm grieving. I have to

know why my son was murdered. Any mother would do the same."

Except maybe not beating a police officer with a cell phone.

"I'm sure. Have the police not been helpful?"

"No. Every time I call, I get the same non-answer. It's an ongoing investigation. I don't know why that Hernandez girl isn't locked up tight. She's been after my son and his money for as long as they'd known one another."

"Hernandez?" I pretended not to know who she was talking about. Playing nice was becoming more difficult by the minute.

"She just opened a bakery here. Tell me who gave her that money? I'm sure it was my son. She was one of his little projects. I still don't understand what he saw in her. As far as I'm concerned, she ruined his life."

My hands fisted under the table. If I punched her in the face for talking trash about one of the best humans I knew, Greg would never let me do this again.

"Your younger son made me cry yesterday with his eulogy."

She blinked. "Levi? We're lucky he didn't mess the whole thing up. Now, that one is a constant disappointment. It's a good thing he has me to guide his life."

The longer she spoke, the easier it was to see why Mort had decided to give a chunk of the company to Lizzie and Jere. I didn't get a sense she knew anything about that.

"I don't know Levi, but it seems like the brothers were close."

She made the ugliest face. "Maybe when they were kids. I

know Levi was furious with him over something at work. He wouldn't tell me what it was."

Sipping the coffee, she beat her long manicured nails on the table.

"How much longer are they going to keep me here?"

"I don't know," I said. "I was just looking for my brother. Let me see what I can find out for you."

"Thank you, dear. It's nice to see someone in this godforsaken town has some manners."

I hurried out. Greg had been watching the whole thing through the interview glass and, I'm sure, recording every word she said. It wouldn't be admissible, but she'd given us a couple of clues.

One of which was that though Levi waxed poetic about his brother, their relationship wasn't ideal.

"Good job," Greg said. He and Lucy both had their arms crossed. Someday I'd figure out what was going on with those two.

"I feel like I should get some sort of gift certificate for not hitting her," I said.

Lucy's eyebrow rose.

"Obviously, I wouldn't do that. But at least we know she wasn't trying to hurt Gran. She was disappointed that she'd been inconvenienced by a coma." That last bit came out bitterly.

"She does have you worked up," Lucy said. "What about the brother?"

"Levi seemed so sincere yesterday. I mean, he was moved to tears and so was I. Maybe it was all for show. She doesn't seem to like him much. This is confusing. Jere said Mort and the family were at odds. Levi says they were the best of friends. And the mom...seems to think the wrong son died. I'm terrible for saying that. Oh, and her hate for Lizzie. Maybe they hired someone to kill her, and it got messed up. That could be why she's so angry. Her detective might actually be a hired killer."

"Hmmm," Lucy said.

Greg stared daggers at the old woman. There was a knock on the door.

"What is it?" Greg asked.

"Sir, the lawyer is here."

Greg took a deep breath. "This should be fun."

"What happened to Jake? Did you make him wait in his office?"

"No, a call came in and he had to run to the station. Do you need one of my guys to drive you to your store?"

I shook my head. "Nah. It's a block and half, I can handle it. Poor George probably thinks I've abandoned him."

As I walked back, I did my best to listen to my gut. It told me the mother wasn't involved, and it was usually right.

Levi and Jere, they made me wonder. I adored Jere. He'd been funny and clever. There was this niggling thing in the back of my brain. He was the assistant; wouldn't he know everything about Mort's life? Maybe, he even knew about the will.

And Levi—had that all been a sham?

One thing was for certain. There were way too many suspects in this case.

Chapter Thirteen

BACK AT THE shop, Mike had already put a list together for shifts to cover Gran and he'd taken George for a walk. My dog was happily chewing on a bone in my office.

"Thank you for the list," I said.

"Maybe, we should send the judge a special thank you since he's covering several of the evening shifts."

I smiled. "It's almost as if he likes her or something."

"Almost." He laughed.

Exhausted, I sat down at my desk and called Lizzie.

Greg said she was fine, but I needed to hear it from her.

"Hello?" It sounded as if she'd been sleeping.

"Did I wake you?"

She yawned. "I haven't been sleeping so well lately. My mind whirls with what-ifs and whys."

"Do you want to talk about it? Were you scared when you found out his mother was in town?"

"I'm not afraid of her, but I am," she said. "I know that doesn't make sense. I've always thought she was a little unhinged. But now with Mort gone, there's no one to keep her on the right side of crazy. That's mean. We aren't supposed to say things like that, but I don't know what she might do."

After speaking with Mrs. Gallagher, I completely agreed.

"I had a chance to speak with her," I said.

"What?" Lizzie coughed.

"Are you okay?"

"Sorry. I'm surprised after what happened in the church."

"She didn't recognize me at all."

"Did she tell you anything?"

"Not a lot more than she's grieving and that the brothers didn't get along. I'm not sure I believed her."

"I never have," Lizzie said. "Goodness knows what she told her friends about me. I've reached a point where I just don't care. But when she finds out about the money and her house—"

"I would not want to be a fly on that wall."

She laughed but it wasn't a happy sound.

"How are you dealing with the inheritance?"

She snorted. "By pretending it didn't happen. They've already put a lump sum of money in my bank account. It's unreal. This whole situation is. I'm taking the lawyer's advice and taking some time to adjust.

"I've talked to Jere a few times about business stuff. Once the poo hits the fan on Friday, we'll need to make sure the employees feel comfortable with the changes. I keep telling him and myself that it will be messy for a while, but we'll figure it out."

"I have no doubt about that. I'm sorry I woke you up. I won't keep you."

"It's okay. If I'd slept much longer, I wouldn't have been able to do so tonight. That's death for a baker like me."

There was a long pause.

"Oh. My. That was a terrible choice of words." She giggled.

I laughed with her.

"Remember, I'm here. Day or night. I mean it. I'm worried about you. This has been a lot to process."

She sniffed. "I don't know what I'd have done without you. I keep saying it, but I mean it."

I checked the security cameras at the shop and all of them worked well. There were several customers at the checkout, so I went out to help.

When the last of the customers departed, I locked the front door and gathered as much of the gang who was there.

The last thing I could wrap my mind around was organizing something so complicated. "Thank you so much for this," I said to Mike.

"Are you okay?" Don asked. "You seem upset."

I chuckled. "I feel like I've lived ten lifetimes in the last two hours."

"Tell us what we can do to help, Ainsley," Don said. "We're family and you can tell us anything." He didn't say it like he wanted inside info, more like he genuinely wanted to ease my troubles. I loved these people. They were talented and clever; maybe they could help.

"Most of you know what's going on," I said. "I'm sort of desperate to find the killer before he or she can try again with Gran, or the others. The situation is a mess and there are too many suspects, none of whom we can place at the scene the night of the murder. One witness is in a coma and the other is so traumatized she can't remember what happened."

Don shook his head. "Your brother isn't going to like you putting your life in danger."

"I'm not going to do that ever again. I've learned my lesson. Trouble finds me without me looking for it. I was wondering if you guys would sit and talk things out with me."

"Oh, my, gosh. Can we pull out the whiteboard?" Carrie asked. She was so mature that sometimes I forgot she was only sixteen. "I've always wanted to help with one of the cases."

I glanced at her mom, Maria. "Me, too," she said, and then smiled.

"Yes, but you guys have to be sworn to secrecy."

Don, Mike, Carrie and Maria raised their hands as if I were swearing them in.

"We better bring Shannon in," Mike said. "If you leave her out of the process, she's going to be mad at both of us."

He wasn't wrong.

The plus side of inviting my BFF is that she brought a huge container of coffee and treats.

"Peggy's teaching a dance class at the nursing home. She's going to be sorry she missed this," Don said, as he pulled out a croissant from the box. I wasn't sure if he was talking about the treats or that we were discussing the case.

We went upstairs to the biggest classroom and everyone took a seat. The rooms are usually for art or craft classes.

I wrote *Mort Gallagher* at the top of the whiteboard. "His family owns one of the largest food distribution companies in the Southwest." Then I wrote his mom and his brother as branches. "There are arguments within the family over what direction to take the company. As we all know, money can be a great motivator.

"The mom favors the victim, so I don't think she had anything to do with it. But she does not like Lizzie, which we all know is close to impossible. I'm keeping her on the list in case she was trying to knock off our friend, and it was her son who was killed instead."

"That would be some terrible karma," Maria said.

"Agreed," I said.

"What about the brother?" Carrie asked.

"Funny you should mention him." I explained about the eulogy, and then how his mother's comments somewhat contradicted what I'd witnessed.

"It could be sibling rivalry," Maria said. "There's a lot of that at my house. They all think I love the other one best."

Carrie sighed. "Mom, you know I'm the favorite."

Maria hugged her. "You are pretty perfect."

"If the mom pitted them against one another, and it sounds like she did, that is the kind of hate that can build up for years," Mike said. "I'm pretty sure I saw that on a CSI show or maybe an FBI one."

I wrote *sibling rivalry* and added a question mark.

"Then we have the other victims. Gran and Becky might have just been in the wrong place at the wrong time. I have this theory that Gran heard Becky scream, and went to see what was going on in the bakery."

"What was she doing there in the first place?" Don asked. "It's not like her to be walking in the park at night. I mean, Sweet River is one of the safest places in the country, but she could have tripped in the dark."

"She had a date with the judge," Mike chimed in.

"I have a theory that's been rolling around in my head," I said.

"Tell us," Carrie said. "I have one too."

I smiled. "Why don't you share your idea first?"

Her eyes went wide and she glanced at the other adults in the room.

"Go ahead." Maria nudged her.

"From what I've heard, Becky came back to the bakery to get some work done. Then she was surprised by Mr. Gallagher. He might have said something that scared her. But I was thinking, if she had her back to him, maybe he thought she was Ms. Lizzie. They both have long, dark hair and are about the same height."

Well, that was something I hadn't thought about.

"Maybe, he said something as a joke that Ms. Lizzie would have thought was funny, but Becky took it as a threat and panicked."

"Becky remembered him saying something like, 'I'm going to get you, girl,'" I added. Carrie made sense. She hadn't known the victim, so when she saw a big man looming toward her—anyone would have been scared.

"Do you think she hit him with the frying pan?" Mike asked.

"Maybe," Carrie said. "That's where my theory sort of ends, because I don't know how Mrs. Whedon and Becky ended up unconscious in the freezer. My idea was that Mrs. Whedon surprised him, and that's when Becky hit him with the skillet. He'd have to be distracted, right?"

"You are good at this. Yes. Kane told me those iron pans are super heavy," I added. "And he was tall, so to hit him—it would have taken a hard and heavy swing."

"Yeah, but when people are scared or trying to protect others, they can do all sorts of things, right?" Maria chimed in.

"Yes, but there had to be someone else," I said. "If it had been Becky or Gran who hit him, one of them would still be conscious."

"What do you think happened?" Mike asked.

"Carrie's theory is pretty much what I've been thinking. Mort had wanted to talk to Lizzie about something important, but he came into town two days early. I wonder if he thought he might be in danger. Someone could have been following him and used the scene at the bakery as an opportunity."

"They wanted to get him out of the way, and there he was," Don said. "And they probably thought one of the other victims would be targeted as the killer. The question is, who in the family, since they seem to be the main suspects, wanted him dead the most?"

"The brother would get my vote. I don't have a good handle on him," I said.

"Yeah, but what if the brother was trying to win his mother's favor in the family war—what better way to show his loyalty than killing the one who stood in their way?" Mike rubbed his chin.

"Another good point," I said.

"Except, Lizzie said he was always the favorite, and the

mom confirmed it a little while ago."

"You talked to the mother?" Shannon asked. "Why didn't you call me?"

I laughed. "My brother asked me to do it on the spur of the moment. She'd lawyered up, so it wasn't official, but I did get a good sense about the family dynamics. Even if they were at odds, it's obvious she loved her son. But I could also see her lying through her teeth and hiring someone to kill him."

"I'm thinking you didn't like her very much," Carrie said. "You're a great judge of character, except for that one time you let that killer lady stay at your house."

No one bothered to hide their laughter.

"Fair point."

"What's turning around in that brain of yours?" Shannon asked. She was probably working on her own theories. Over the past year and a half, she'd helped me on several cases.

I pursed my lips. "The mom mentioned she had her detective checking things out. It made me think it was someone they used often. The family might have been trying to get dirt on Mort or find out what he was up to. But why now? The argument of theirs had been going on for years."

My phone buzzed in my pocket, but I ignored it. Then it buzzed again. I pulled it out to see who was calling.

"What's wrong? You have your *why is this person calling me* face."

"It's not a call. It's a text."

"From who?" Shannon asked.

"Becky."

The text said: *I think I know who killed Lizzie's friend.*

Chapter Fourteen

I CHECKED THE security camera at the back door from my phone and Becky was there with a deputy. After unlocking it, I pushed the heavy door open.

"Hi, Ainsley, thanks for helping me pick out a gift for my friend," Becky said quickly. "I know you guys are closed. I hope you don't mind."

She blinked back tears. She didn't want the deputy to know why she was really here.

"Not at all. We just closed up, so you have the whole store to yourself."

"Thank you," she said as she stepped in.

"Deputy Carter, you are welcome to come inside and wait in the break room," I offered.

He glanced from me to the young girl. "If it's okay with you, I'd like to run to the Dairy Queen and pick up some lunch. With all the excitement today there wasn't time. That is if you'll promise to lock up after I leave."

"Of course," I said.

"Becky, would you like something from the DQ?" the officer asked.

"I'm good for now, but thank you," she said sweetly, but I noticed she didn't turn around. Poor thing was barely keeping it together. Had she seen the killer and remembered everything?

He left and I locked the door as promised.

"Why don't you come sit down in the break room and tell me what's going on," I said. "I have coffee and tea, if you want some."

Tears fell on her cheeks and my heart ached for her.

"Hey, you're safe. We'll figure it out whatever it is."

"Sorry," she said, on a sob.

"It's all right. I promise I will help you no matter what is going on. We're friends. I'd do anything for you. Hold on and let me grab some tissues." I seemed to be doing that a lot lately.

When I came back, she had her head down on her arms.

"Here you go." I handed them to her.

"Thanks." She wiped her sweet face.

"Pull off the Band-Aid and tell me what happened. Did you see someone who reminded you of that night?"

"I keep having flashes and I feel something heavy in my hands," Becky said in a sob. "I wonder if I feel so miserable because part of my brain knows I killed Lizzie's friend. Maybe, I even hurt Mrs. Whedon because I couldn't tell the good from the bad. I started to turn myself in to the deputy, but then—I just wanted to talk to you about it. You're smart at this kind of stuff. I overheard Shannon telling Lizzie that you're a really good investigator."

I smiled and patted her hand. "I'll have to tell Shannon thanks for that." Of course, knowing her and the rest of the gang, they were listening from the top of the stairs. There was nothing I could do about that now.

"Tell me why you think you could have done it, and I'll

explain why I don't think you did."

Her brows came together in surprise. "You don't?"

"Nope. But you explain to me what these flashes are. Try closing your eyes again and piece together those moments."

Her hand reached out, like she was going through the actions. "I open the freezer door and I have the jar of oil we use. It's a special blend that keeps the dough from drying out. But I hear his voice. 'I'm gonna get you, girl.'" She said it roughly, imitating a man's voice. Her body shook from head to toe, as if she were truly experiencing it in the moment.

I squeezed her hand. "You're safe now. You don't have to worry about anything. I'm right here with you," I said softly. Part of me was worried that this young girl needed a very real therapist to lead her through this. I had no idea if I was doing more harm than good. I prayed I was helping.

"I screamed loud. When I turned, he was smiling and then he seemed surprised. 'You're not Lizzie.'

'Why do you want to hurt Lizzie!' I screamed at him. I needed to find a weapon. There was no way I'd let him hurt Lizzie. She's my boss but also my best friend. I turned out of his arms and went for the freezer. There are big bowls stored in there and they are heavy.

"There's another voice yelling and this time it isn't me. Maybe they want to hurt Lizzie, too. But when I go to get a big bowl, I see the iron frying pan. And then I'm falling backward. I feel myself going down and then it's dark."

She opened her eyes. "He was surprised but I don't think he meant to hurt me," she said. "I feel awful. Maybe the frying pan is a metaphor or something. I watched a bunch of serial killer shows the last few days and that can happen."

I would have made fun of her television viewing habits, but TV and books were how I'd learned my detective skills—such as they are.

"Okay, a couple of things. Your fingerprints weren't on the frying pan," I said. "It had been wiped clean. So, someone did that after they murdered him. Since you were most likely out cold in the freezer, no pun intended, you didn't do that. Do you remember anything about Mrs. Whedon being there?"

She closed her eyes again. "When I first woke up, someone was on top of me. It was dark and cold, and I had no idea where I was, or how I got there. I was having trouble breathing because of the person on top of me.

"When you opened the freezer door, the light came on, and you know the rest. How is Mrs. Whedon? I heard the deputies talking at the bakery that some woman got in her room."

This sweet girl had been through so much. She was just out of high school and going to college in the fall. She had her whole life in front of her.

"She's doing well, though I need her to wake up. I'll feel better about life then. Becky, you didn't hurt anyone. You were just in the wrong place at the wrong time. I'm grateful you weren't hurt worse than the bump on the head."

"Me too. I feel like a hundred years of life have happened this last week."

I smiled. "I just said the same sort of thing to my friends."

"I've been in this horrible daze. When I'm at work, I'm

so busy I don't have time to think about it. But when I go back to my apartment, it's all I can think about. I'm grateful Lizzie insisted I stay with her until all of this is over. She keeps busy all the time, trying out new recipes.

"I've been worried the last few days that I killed her friend. And here I am, staying in her house. It got to me today."

"How is she doing? I haven't seen her since yesterday."

"She's playing a lot of songs from the nineties and I've caught her crying a couple of times. It ripped my soul open when the flashes started. She's so sad and it doesn't feel right. A week ago, she was the happiest person I ever met. If I hurt her friend, she'd never forgive me."

"You didn't hurt anyone." At least, I didn't think so now. "You've been so brave this week. All of that happened to you, and you went back to work. My heart hurts for you that you've been holding on to all of this. I wish you'd come to me sooner. If you remember anything else, I'm here for you."

Her shoulders dropped and she sighed. "I feel better. Like, so much."

"I'm glad."

"I have two favors to ask. If that's okay."

"Uh, sure."

"One, do I need to go to the police and tell them what I remembered? Or is that something you could tell your brother for me?"

I chewed on my lip. "I'll let him know, but you will probably have to go in and make a statement. It's important for them to have all of the facts when they make a case against the person who did all of this. What's the second thing?"

"I know you guys invited me to the girls' night thingy, but I'd really like to go home to the ranch. Riding is how I get out of my head."

I didn't blame her. "Again, we'll need to talk to Greg. If you want, I can see if he's available now."

She went white again.

"Don't worry. I'll be here with you. And I give him a hard time because he's my brother, but he's very fair and kind. It's what makes him a great sheriff. But if you mention I said that I'll never speak to you again."

She laughed, and her color came back.

"Now, let's go find a candle or something, so the deputy thinks you really did need a gift, and my brother will believe I bugged you to death until you finally told me."

"Thank you, Ainsley. For everything."

"No problem."

While we were looking around the shop, I texted Shannon.

Sneak out the back.

I was certain she heard our whole conversation and wouldn't want to be here when Greg arrived.

She sent me a thumbs-up.

The deputy showed up with his lunch not long after that and sat in the break room and ate it, while I explained that I needed to talk to Greg.

"I'll call for him. He's at the station. They got a lead on a car they think the suspect might have used."

I was glad Becky was in the bathroom washing her face.

Her nerves were bad enough.

Using his walkie-talkie, he reached out to Greg, who must have been close because he was at the back door in less than a minute. Followed by Jake.

"You never texted me to pick you up, so I thought I'd stop by to make sure you were okay."

He didn't seem that worried and I figured Shannon had texted him to come over and be a buffer with Greg. Though, technically, it wasn't my fault this time that a witness spilled the beans.

George woofed, as if to say it was food time. He'd been hanging out in my office all this time, and had just woken up.

"Would you mind taking George for a walk? I promised Becky I'd stay with her while she talks to Greg and the deputy. I mean, if that's okay with you, Sheriff?" I used my polite and respectful voice.

"Becky, is that what you want?" Greg asked her gently.

She nodded.

"I'll take George out, and figure out some dinner. Greg, do you need something?" Jake asked.

"I haven't had lunch yet," he said. "I'm about to take the deputy's fries in as evidence." Everyone laughed, including Becky. My brother was good at reading a scene. Helping Becky relax was one of his tactics, and it worked.

The deputy passed his fries over and Greg took a couple.

"I'll pick up dinner. Becky, do you want anything?" Jake asked her.

She blushed. Jake did that to women of all ages. "No thank you. I'm too nervous to eat."

"Don't be," Greg said. "You are helping us. Every detail matters."

"That's what Ainsley said."

"Sometimes, my sister knows what she's talking about."

We all laughed.

BY THE TIME Jake returned with George, Greg had finished questioning Becky.

"Becky was hoping she could maybe go home to be with her parents this weekend? Her horses are there and she loves to ride."

"As long as the deputy is with you, I don't have a problem with it."

"I'm really grateful." Again, I hate to admit it, but my brother is smart. He probably understood better than any of us that she had been through more than any young girl should have.

"Deputy, talk with her parents. Do you mind staying with her until I can figure out something with the local law enforcement?"

"Sheriff, I don't mind and I'll talk to the chief over there. He and I are fishing buddies."

After Becky gave me a tight hug, she and the deputy left.

Jake put several bags from Dairy Queen on the table. We'd been eating so healthy and my mouth was watering at the prospect of fries and a cheeseburger.

"This one's yours, Ains." He handed me a bag. There were no fries. Two chicken breasts were wrapped in lettuce. I didn't want to seem ungrateful, but man, I really wanted a burger.

"Thanks for this," Greg said as he pulled out two triple cheeseburgers and two orders of fries.

Ugh. Men. They could eat whatever they wanted and not worry about blood sugar or gaining weight. At least, the men around me could. It wasn't fair.

"She came to you," Greg said. It was more of a statement rather than a question.

I shrugged. "I guess she felt more comfortable with me."

"I appreciate you calling me in," Greg said.

He was being unusually nice. Maybe he was just tired. There were lines around his eyes that weren't normally there.

We ate in silence for a bit, except for George who was gulping down his burgers.

"Why do I get the feeling you want to ask me something?" Greg asked.

"I *am* wondering if there's a way we can find out who has a tattoo on their neck," I said. "I don't know a lot about Levi, the brother, other than Lizzie says he wasn't the favorite son and the mom said the same thing."

"The mom actually picked a favorite?" Jake's eyes were wide with amazement. He was so kind, thoughtful, and fair, that it wasn't plausible to him that someone could be so cruel.

"Our friend Jere says he has a stick up his butt. I'm just trying to think about who had the most to gain by getting rid of Mort."

"Who is Jere?" Jake asked. He frowned.

"Are you jealous?"

His eyebrow went up.

I laughed.

Greg snorted.

"Don't worry. I'm not his type or gender. He's funny, and I think he and Lizzie are becoming great friends, which is good, since they'll be running the company together. Have you guys been able to get into the business files, yet?"

"We're waiting on a court order. The county judge there wouldn't help us out, so we had to get help from the federal court."

"Hmmm."

"What?" Greg put his burger down.

"Jere told us that the family owned the town and everyone in it. That would make sense."

"Do you think the victim and Jere were lovers?" Greg asked.

I hadn't really thought about Jere that way. "I have no idea but I can ask him. He's pretty open about stuff."

Greg smirked. "That's kind of my job."

"But I might be able to get more out of him."

"Except, you're supposed to be sequestered in town."

"How do you feel about a little road trip? I've been thinking about getting a tattoo."

Greg knocked over his soda, which had a lid and didn't spill much. But I was worried Jake might have to give himself the Heimlich he was coughing so hard. I pounded on his back.

"A tattoo?" Jake said hoarsely.

"What do you guys have against tattoos? You both have them."

Greg and Jake just stared at each other. Then Greg rolled his eyes.

"You've never mentioned it," Jake said carefully.

"There are a thousand different tattoo parlors in Austin. It is the coolest city in the world. But how many would there be down where the family lives? I mean, if it's one of them. Or someone who works for them, maybe I could check it out. I have this feeling if I see it, I'll know what it is."

"You are not going to tattoo parlors by yourself," Greg said.

"She doesn't like it when you say it that way," Jake interjected. "I think what Greg means is: they aren't always the nicest places with the best clientele. There are some upscale ones. Your best bet might be checking out their stuff online."

"I'll do some research tonight, so I can go through and see if there is a font that is similar. Maybe I'll see it online."

I'm a terrible person. I had no intention of asking either of them to go. This was definitely a girls' sort of thing. I couldn't get Lizzie away from her watcher without Greg finding out, but I had a feeling Shannon and Jasmine would be all over this.

And I really had been thinking about a tattoo. Maybe because it is very un-me. But I had a big birthday coming up, and I had a new life that I loved. I just thought it might be fun to document this time of my life.

I also had a grave aversion to needles and pain.

"She's doing that thing," Jake said. "Where she says one thing, but she's thinking something else."

Darn that man. He really did pay attention. "Not at all. That's my *I wonder where I should start researching* face."

I'd promised Jake to never lie to him. Like I said, I'm a horrible person. But I would do anything to keep my friends safe, even if it meant getting inked.

Chapter Fifteen

MY FRIEND SHANNON is the sweetest, most manipulative human in the world. By Wednesday afternoon, she'd convinced Jake, Mike, and Greg that she was taking me out for a pre-birthday bash. One she'd had planned for months. She even blindfolded me to make it look real. And "kidnapped" me from the shop.

The kicker was she even convinced them to let Lizzie come with us. She told them she had a hotel suite in Austin and that we were going to shop, eat, and drink margaritas until we fell down.

We were in Mike's big truck so that we all fit comfortably, and were headed out of town.

"Do you think one of them will follow?" Jasmine asked. "They are all very protective of Ainsley."

"They better not," Shannon said. "And, technically, I didn't lie once. We are going to go shopping—just for tattoos instead of what they think. We'll eat Mexican food and drink margaritas. There is this great place that's near one of the tattoo shops Ainsley sent in her message."

"Oh, I have a tattoo shop to add," Lizzie said. "Jere called me back. He said if we go there, to call him. He knows the owner and can get us a deal. It's a popular spot with the locals. I mean, we aren't actually getting tattoos. But you get it."

Deadly Tattoos was in a strip mall that had Taco Bonita at one end and a laundromat at the other.

"So you can get a tattoo, grab dinner and do your laundry at the same time," Jasmine said. "That's some clever bundling."

"Do you think they do walk-ins?" I asked. "Some tattoo artists are booked up for months ahead of time. When I was doing my research I learned that."

Shannon shrugged. "This doesn't look like the kind of place that is booked out for months ahead. Though, I'm the last to judge. I had mine done in a tent at spring break on the beach."

We all turned to look at her. "I've known you how long and you have a tattoo?"

"I don't talk about it very often because I'm embarrassed."

"Oh, now you have to show us," Jasmine said.

"Yes. Show us. Show us. Show us," Lizzie sang. It was good to see her smiling again.

"Y'all, I'm gonna need some margaritas before that happens."

We all laughed.

"At least tell us what it is," I said.

She sighed dramatically. "If I tell you, promise that none of you will share the information?"

"Everything that happens tonight is under the code of silence," I said. "If the guys find out what we're doing, I'll never hear the end of it."

"It's a dolphin," she said. "And not, an oh, that's a pretty dolphin. It's super cheesy. Consider this my public service announcement: Never get a tattoo on a beach during a party."

"Noted," I said.

We climbed out of the truck and headed inside. The sun was still bright outside, so I blinked and tried to focus on the dark shop. It was nicer than I'd imagined and super clean. There was a young girl, who was dressed like an anime character, at the front counter and she smiled and waved us closer.

"Are you ladies looking for tattoos?"

We nodded in unison. I tried to not bust out laughing. We had no idea what we were doing.

"It's her birthday." Shannon pointed to me. "It's coming up and she's been talking about a tattoo for a while. We looked stuff up online, but we thought maybe it would be a good idea to come in and actually look at the art. She still can't decide what she wants. And we have no idea how much they even cost."

The girl's smile widened. "You came to a great place for your first tattoos. My dad, Juan Lelo, owns the shop. He started in New York and has worked all over the world. He won't let me put his trophies out, but he's won a lot.

"But the cool thing for you guys is the last Sunday of every month he teaches a class about how to find your perfect tattoo. He says the art you share on your body is an expression of you. He teaches people how to figure out what that might be. It's also online, but I think you get more out of the class if you're in person. Though, he's my dad, so I might be biased."

Whatever my expectations had been about a tattoo shop, this was nowhere close. Even if I hadn't been thinking about one, I would have signed up. She was quite the salesperson.

"Can I ask you a really rude question?" Lizzie said.

The girl shrugged.

"How old are you?"

The girl laughed. "I'm twenty-one. I know with the pigtails I look like I'm twelve. I'm finally old enough to learn the craft, so I'm studying with my dad. Even though I feel like I've been doing it all my life."

I thought maybe she was sixteen.

"I'm glad this was our first stop," I said. "I will definitely look into that class. I was wondering if we could look at some of the shop's work. I can't decide if I want lettering, or to maybe get my Great Dane on my shoulder."

"Oh. I love Great Danes. We have a punt and kick poodle right now. That's what my dad says. But don't worry. He treats that dog better than me most days. I love big dogs. Let me show you some examples."

We stood there looking at all the books. I found one that was a dog paw, but had the dog's face in the paw. It was a work of art and had been done by her dad. If I ever did decide to do one, I'd definitely come to him.

Unfortunately, I didn't see anything that looked like the tip of the tattoo, I'd seen.

TWO HOURS LATER, we'd visited all the shops on my list. None of them were as cool as the first one, and the people who worked in the other shops didn't seem to care. I was going to email Juan and tell him how amazing his daughter was.

"I'm so hungry," Shannon said. "Let's eat before we hit the last one."

Lizzie asked Jere to meet us at the restaurant and he agreed.

We did a giant fajita platter with every kind of meat and fish, and had several pitchers of margaritas. Well, they did. Shannon and I were working.

"Y'all are so sweet to invite me to girls' night," Jere said. "I brought you a little gift, Ainsley."

He handed me a big Sephora bag.

"You didn't have to do this. I'm just glad you could join us."

"Girl, anytime I get to stop at Sephora, I do. I love me some product. I'm very bad at the one for you, one for me sort of thing."

"Me too," I said. "I'm worse when I'm holiday shopping. My friends will be like, I love those earrings. And I'm thinking, 'Good, because you're getting the same thing in a different color.'"

Everyone laughed.

"She's not lying," Shannon said. "But she's got great taste when it comes to gifts."

"I had kind of a day, so I appreciate the invite."

"Oh, no." Lizzie touched his arm. "Tell us about it."

He waved his hand. "I don't want to ruin the fun with mean work stuff."

"If it's business, maybe I can help," Jasmine said.

"She's a big-time consultant and owns half of Houston," Shannon blurted out.

Jasmine snorted, and Lizzie and Jere's eyes went wide.

"Sorry," Shannon said. "She hates it when people find out—I need to just shut up now. And I can't even blame the margaritas. Jasmine, forgive me, please."

"Eh. We're all friends here," she said. "So tell us what happened."

"Well, the day after the funeral, Levi tried to come in and fire everyone who had been loyal to his brother. It wasn't him though, his mom was behind it all. Levi, well, he can be a stuffed shirt, but he's a nice guy.

"I called the lawyer during the drama, and she called some of the board members, who put a stop to it." He glanced at Lizzie. "Do they know what happened yet?" He waved toward the rest of the table.

"They don't have a lot of secrets between the three of them," she said.

Jasmine and Shannon had been at the dinner when I talked to my brother about everything.

"The gist is, Lizzie and I inherited fifty-one percent of the company where I work," Jere whispered. "But we can't say anything until the reading of the will, which is on Friday. All heck is going to break loose when the family finds out about me and Lizzie. Meanwhile, Mom-Devil tried to come in and go through papers in Mort's office. I had a feeling after the other day, that she'd try something like that. So, I put all the important stuff in the safe, and conveniently forgot the code. At least, until Friday."

"That does sound like a mess," Jasmine says. "Let me

know, if you need help. In my former life, before taking over my family's company, I was a management consultant."

"We might just do that," Lizzie said. "I really wanted no part of this, but I want to keep Mort's legacy alive."

Jere sighed dramatically. "Once the poo hits the fan on Friday, I'd love to know how to navigate the craziness that will be our office. I might call in sick on Friday, just to avoid the initial explosion of hate."

I loaded a fajita.

"I wouldn't blame you," Lizzie said. "One thing about getting divorced was that I never had to see his family again. They never approved of me, and his mom—to this day—swears I'm the reason he came out."

We all laughed.

"Like we have a choice with that sort of thing," Jere said. "I was lucky with my mom. I was dating girls in high school. I came home one night depressed. And my mom said, 'Hon, you're gay. You might not be able to admit it yet, but you are. If you date boys, I think you'll be happier.'"

"Awwww, that's so sweet," Shannon said.

"And unusual," Jere said. "She was a teacher and she just knew. It took me another six months to admit she was right. I was lucky but most kids aren't."

"That reminds me," Lizzie said. "Do you know if Mort was dating anyone? I was thinking about that on the way here. They might not even know he's gone. That would be such a terrible feeling."

Jere stared down at his fajita for a moment and our table grew quiet.

"Are you okay?" I asked.

He shook his shoulders and then smiled. "Sorry, sometimes I forget he's gone. I'm pretty sure he was between commitments. I don't remember him going out that much the last couple of months." His voice had gone somber, as if he were remembering something terribly sad.

"Did you guys date?" I asked. Everyone around me gasped. His reaction at the funeral and the look on his face made me wonder.

He shook his head. "We were friends who went out a lot together."

That was a very non-answer.

"I say we do some shots of tequila and go see a man about tattoos," he joked.

"Hear. Hear." Lizzie lifted her margarita glass. She gave me a look though that showed she was just as curious about Jere's relationship with Mort.

I couldn't imagine him killing anyone. But maybe he had an idea who might have done it. He was definitely upset about something.

And I was determined to find out that something before the end of the night.

Chapter Sixteen

AT THE TATTOO shop, which was much swankier than the other places we'd been, we sat in the lobby going through the books. None of us was going to get a tattoo, well maybe Jere. He'd told us on the way over that most of his legs were covered and parts of his back.

He was pretty drunk, actually, most of our party was. And we were loud. The receptionist kept laughing at Jere and his antics. They seemed to know one another fairly well.

"Do you want Tina tonight?" she asked Jere. "Or are you doing black and white?"

He turned to face us. "Tina does the best color work in Texas," he said, and maybe slurred the state we live in a little.

"Since you've been drinking, you will have to sign a waiver that says you can't sue if you have regrets in the morning."

"That makes a lot of sense," I said. "Do you have a lot of parties like ours?"

She shrugged. "We do. Some folks need a bit of courage from their friends. They also come in sometimes to do group tattoos. But drinking isn't actually good when you get tattoos because alcohol thins the blood."

"Oh. My. Gosh. We should totally get a group one," Shannon said.

I laughed. I'd promised to drive Mike's truck because she wanted to do shots with the rest of them. But after one shot, she was pretty much done. Probably had something to do with the fact she got up at three every morning to get her coffee shop open.

"Maybe, next time," I said. "I'm still trying to figure out what I want."

"How many artists do you have here?" Lizzie asked.

"All seven are working tonight. Did you have something in mind?"

Lizzie handed over a napkin with the cutest three-layer cake and a unicorn topper. "I'm a baker," Lizzie said. "This was one of the cakes that helped me launch my business."

"I had no idea you could draw like that," I said. The cake could have been something in a picture book.

Lizzie shrugged. "I make most of my own templates so they are original to my bakery. It's just something I picked up along the way."

"Tina would be great with this one," the woman at the counter said. "Do you mind if I take it back to get a quote for you?"

"Go ahead." Lizzie grinned and then did the silent squeal.

Jasmine and Shannon were looking through the books with Jere, so I pulled Lizzie aside.

"I just want to make sure—you're a grown woman—it's just tequila can sometimes make people do things they regret."

She laughed and then hugged me. "Thank you for looking out for me but I'm fine. I'm not drunk. I have a rule about that. And I've wanted to get this tattoo since I opened the bakery, but I've been busy. After everything that happened, it just feels like the right time. Mort loved this sort of thing. Something crazy on the spur of the moment. He was right—time does go by way too fast."

I smiled. "Okay."

She glanced back. "I think there might have been something between them," she said. "I can't tell if they were dating, but there's something more personal there. He cared about Mort, maybe it was like a brother, or a lover. Shannon told me you have a way of getting people to tell their darkest secrets."

Why did everyone think empathy was so hard? That was my big secret way of interviewing people—and being kind.

"Oh. Yeah?"

She nodded. "There were things he said a few days ago, and tonight, that were the same sort of thoughts Mort had. And that look on his face at dinner. If that wasn't a broken heart, I don't know what was."

That meant I hadn't been imagining the feelings Jere had for his boss. If Lizzie saw it as well, then there was definitely something going on, but why would he lie about it? I thought it was odd that Mort would leave so much money to his assistant.

Then again, why had he left so much to Lizzie? I hadn't had a chance to read the letters he gave them.

"I need to ask you something personal," I said. "I hope you don't mind."

She smiled at me. "You can ask me anything."

"I'm curious what Mort's letter said."

She shrugged. "Pretty much what I told you. He said that he had trouble trusting anyone, especially his family. He'd worked hard to turn the company into a respectable organization. That his dad had done some bad things in the past, but he had cleared the decks."

"Do you know what his father had done? Maybe someone took out the debt on Mort."

She shook her head. "That would have been years ago. His dad passed away about two years after our divorce. I remember Jere saying that things were uglier than ever with his family. Right after that, he took over the company. He'd been working as VP of something. Gosh, it was all so long ago. I wish I could get it straight for you."

I put my hands on her shoulders. "Don't worry about it. I mean it. But if you remember something about the family, let me know. Right now, they seem like the most likely suspects."

She chewed on her lip. "As bad as things got, I can't see his mom doing anything to hurt him. I keep saying that but she had him on a pedestal."

"What about his brother?"

"Mort was always worried his dad was a bad influence on Levi, especially when it came to taking out his anger. He was a cruel man.

"Mort fought back and eviscerated the old man with words, but Levi would take it. That said, Levi and I have always gotten along—even after the divorce. He's a great guy, even though he's been through a lot. I feel sorry for him. Jere didn't think he was strong enough to go against his mom, but I think he might have if he'd been given the chance."

"One more question; do you know if Levi had any tattoos?"

"I don't know," she said.

I started to text Greg, and then thought better of it. If I started asking questions about the family, he'd get suspicious. I was supposed to be out on a spectacular birthday bash.

"Lizzie?" the receptionist called.

I went up to the desk with her.

The receptionist said, "Here's the quote, and she had a cancellation. So, if you want to do it tonight she's ready for you."

"Do you take credit cards?" Lizzie asked.

"Yes, ma'am."

"Good luck," I said.

Lizzie tugged on my arm. "Can my friend come back with me?"

"Sure," the woman said.

I'd watched tattoo shows on television, but I'd never been up close.

As we went back to the studio, we passed a guy with a man bun, who called out Jere's name.

"I guess he's getting one, too," I said.

"Yeah, he decided to get one to honor Mort," Lizzie said.

"That's sweet," I said. Maybe, Jere wasn't as picky as I was about a tattoo. But it seemed to me he and Mort were much closer than I'd been led to believe.

She motioned for me to sit on a stool beside a leather lounge chair that moved up and down.

"I'm Tina," she said. She had bubble gum-pink hair and

a tattoo necklace of stars and moons.

"I'm Lizzie, and this is the birthday girl, Ainsley." Lizzie lay back on the lounger.

"You aren't getting a tattoo?" the artist asked.

"I still can't decide what I want."

"Makes sense. There's a guy, he's one of the best artists in the world, who teaches a class about that. I'll write down his name for you."

"Thank you." I wondered if she was talking about the same guy from earlier.

"Now, Lizzie, where did you want to put this adorable cake?"

"I was thinking my upper arm."

"Is this your first tattoo?"

Lizzie nodded.

"That's a good spot then, because there are fewer nerves."

"Will it hurt?"

"Not if I do it right," Tina joked. "You'll feel some pressure. And your arm may get a little sore. There's a lot of color in this, which takes a little longer. Are you ready?"

"I am," she said.

Across the studio, Jere took off his shirt. For someone who appeared so slim, he was incredibly fit. His muscles were well defined, and he had an eight-pack.

I did not see that coming.

And then he turned around and it was all I could do not to gasp.

Chapter Seventeen

I FUMBLED FOR my phone in my purse, and then quickly took a picture. I prayed no one saw me. Shannon and Jasmine were still out in the lobby of the tattoo parlor. I texted them, and not long after, their names were called, as well.

Shannon was following one of the tattoo artists, and Jasmine another.

"Are you both getting tattoos?" I asked.

"Yes," they said together and at the same time stared over at the lounger where Jere was lying on his stomach. Shannon's eyes went wide as she glanced back at me.

Were we in the room with a killer? Jere fit the body size of the man I'd seen in the park. He was well over six feet. But it had been dark under the trees, and I'd been on a slight incline.

My stomach churned. So many things were adding up. The tattoo with the serif, the fact that he was getting another to represent his former boss and friend.

Did he have an alibi? I tried to think back to our previous conversations but I hadn't asked him where he'd been that night. I racked my brain trying to figure out a way I could do that without making him suspicious.

"Excuse me a minute," I said to Lizzie. "I want to check

on Jere."

I sat down on a stool next to his lounger. "You doing okay, buddy?"

He had his head turned toward me and smiled. "Yep. Are you the only one who isn't getting one tonight?"

"I feel like a nerd," I said. "But I just can't decide what I want. I was curious about what you were doing?"

"I'm getting '4-ever' under 'Bros,'" he said, as if that explained everything.

"Cool. Did you get the Bros one here?"

"Nope. I was in Mexico with Mort and Levi, and there was a hurricane. We'd all been there for a convention, and the tension between the both of them was really uncomfortable. But the storm sort of made us all grateful we'd survived the night. The next day, we got the tattoos. They made me an honorary brother."

Ugh. This case was more confusing than ever.

"That's so sweet," I said. "I figured with all of the stuff you'd said, about the fight for control, that they weren't very close."

He sighed.

"Dude," the artist said. "No big breaths." He glared at me.

"Sorry," Jere said.

"You know how family is. They loved one another, but the Mom-Devil influence was strong. I have a feeling, before all of this happened, that they were going to try another power play—or she was. Levi and Mort were getting along pretty good, until recently.

"I'm not looking forward to Friday. I guess, now, it will

be mine and Lizzie's problem."

If the brother had the same tattoo, maybe he'd been the one there that night. He and Jere's builds were similar.

"You weren't by chance around when the family found out about Mort's death?"

"No," he said. "I went home and crashed Friday night. I'd been working with the boss on some big reports for the upcoming board meeting. He said he was going out of town to see a friend and for me to get some rest. It wasn't until I saw the news on Saturday night that I knew what happened."

He was home with no alibi, and who knew were the brother was. I had to call Greg, but not tonight. Maybe they'd finally been able to get alibis at least.

Two hours later, everyone but me had tattoos. I'd been fascinated by the different techniques. My friends were so excited and the art was gorgeous.

After we dropped Jere off at his apartment, we headed to the hotel. It was past midnight and we were all exhausted.

The suite was amazing, but we were all too tired to enjoy it. Lizzie passed out on the couch as soon as she sat down. Jasmine helped me straighten her out, and we put a blanket that had been draped over one of the chairs on her.

I went to see which room Shannon had picked out, and she'd fallen asleep on a chaise longue by the balcony doors.

"I guess we get the beds," Jasmine said, and she draped another blanket over our friend.

"I know Shannon got a coffee cup on her wrist. What did you get?" I whispered as we headed down the hallway to the bedrooms.

She pulled her T-shirt down and lifted the bandage over her heart.

I'm sentimental, and my eyes watered. There were two candles, one with 'dad,' the other with 'sis.' Jasmine made candles in her spare time, and those two family members had been killed in tragic circumstances.

I waved a hand in front of my eyes so I didn't cry. "That is so sweet and meaningful," I said.

"It just came to me when I was standing there in the lobby. It felt right, and I love the way it came out. I don't think I'll have regrets in the morning."

"You shouldn't. It's gorgeous. You have a meaningful piece of beautiful art there."

"Thanks. Night, Ainsley."

"Night, Jas. See you in the morning."

In the bedroom, I sat on the edge of the bed and stared out onto the Austin skyline.

Jasmine's case reminded me of just how twisted family dynamics could be. If Jere was right, and there was about to be a power play, what better way to get rid of the stumbling block, than to kill him?

Of course, Jere might have been covering for himself. It was such a jumbled mess. Though, I still couldn't imagine him killing anyone.

But I'd been surprised before.

What I needed was access to my brother's files and a distraction. Maybe not in that order.

Access to the family interviews was a necessity. I had this gut feeling I'd be able to tell if they were guilty.

Whatever was at stake, the person might kill again and my gut, which I always trusted, made me feel like we were on borrowed time. We had to find the killer before he or she found us.

Chapter Eighteen

THE NEXT AFTERNOON, Shannon dropped me off at my shop. With the festival beginning the next week, we were more crowded than normal. I jumped in to help where needed. By closing time, I was dead on my feet. But I had three stops to make.

The first was to check on Gran. I was grateful to see that it was like trying to get into Fort Knox to see her. When I was finally allowed access, Carrie was reading out loud to her.

"She likes thrillers and so do I," Carrie said, as she held up the book. What sixteen-year-old girl reads to an unconscious curmudgeon? Carrie did. She really was an amazing girl. I was reminded of that almost every day.

"I didn't know you had a shift tonight," she said.

"I don't. I just wanted to check on her and it's good to see color in her face. She's been pretty pale lately."

"I did some research about that," Carrie said. "There's a therapist who comes in twice a day and moves her arms and stuff around. That gets the blood and oxygen flowing. It's good for the brain. She's been twitching a lot tonight. I'm hoping that means her synapses are firing back up."

"Me too," I said. "Thank you for doing this."

"I like hanging out with her. I like it better when she's

awake and shares her stories. She's had a very interesting life. Mine is so boring."

"But you still have a lot of life to live," I said. "That totally sounded like a greeting card."

We laughed.

"Do you want to stay?"

"I'd like to, but I have some errands to run. Are you okay in here by yourself?"

"Yep. During the summer, it's nice to get away from my brothers at home. It's why I've been working at the shop so much. They are loud and crazy. I love them, but this is a treat getting to sit and read."

"All right. Well, I guess I'll be going."

"Uh. There is one thing I need to tell you," she said. She frowned and I couldn't imagine what could be so bad.

"You've been really busy, so I wanted to let you know that we're almost done with the float," she said. "I hope you don't mind."

I flattened my hand against my forehead. "I totally forgot about the float."

"I figured. Mom and Don said it was okay to move forward. I had to make some changes to the original design because it was too elaborate for the time we have. I'm pretty sure you're going to like it."

"I'm sure I will. I owe you, Carrie. Anything you want, it's yours."

She smiled. "You don't owe me anything. It's our shop and we all work together. But…later this year I'll be sending out college applications and I'd love to get a recommendation letter. I mean, that's not why I've been doing all of this."

I believed her. Like her mom, Maria, Carrie had the loveliest heart.

"Say no more. It's the very least I could do. I'll write you a glowing one."

"Yay. Thanks."

"We should restart book club in the fall," I said.

"I'm old enough to go now. I think that's a great idea. I love talking about books. I keep changing my mind about careers, but I think I might want to be a doctor. I've been going through her charts and asking questions. Then I look it up to make sure I understand what they're saying."

"You, my friend, can do anything you set your brilliant mind to. Thanks for looking after Gran. You are officially my favorite human for the 400th time."

"Ditto," she said.

I loved this kid.

NEXT, I WAS headed to the station. It was only four in the afternoon, and I hoped Greg wasn't in the office. Distracting Kevin was often easier than doing the same thing to my brother. I had my hand on the glass door, when my phone rang.

"Hey, Jake," I answered.

"Ains, I need you to come to the vet clinic. I'm here with George, and..."

I didn't hear the rest. I just took off running as fast as I could. It was two blocks down and then another one to the right of the park.

My heart pounded. *Please be okay. Please be okay*, I chanted.

By the time I arrived, I was sweating and sobbing like a child.

No one was in the lobby. I dinged the bell. Maybe a little harder than I should, while I reached for some tissues to blot my face.

Poor George. If anything happened to him, I—I couldn't go there. He was going to be okay. For a dog that ate just about everything, he had a sensitive stomach. I hoped he hadn't eaten Mr. Squirrel. It wouldn't be for lack of trying.

"Please. God. Let him be okay."

I dinged the bell. Still no one answered. I turned around in a circle.

There was a sign on the door. "Please bring your pets to the back of the building."

I ran back and around, and then stopped. There were tons of people there holding champagne glasses and milling around. A party? Didn't they know George was sick?

I glanced around and I was about to scream, when Jake came jogging toward me. He was dressed in a nice button-down and his jeans.

"Where's George?" I cried. "Why are you at a party?"

"George is here," he said. He pulled me to the side of the building.

"But vet. George." I couldn't quite get the words out.

He yanked a handkerchief out of his pocket and blotted my face. "George is fine. You hung up on me so I didn't get to finish. He's not sick. He's happy. Do you understand me?"

Everything was a blur.

"Breathe, Ainsley. Did you eat today?"

"Why are you asking me about food? I want to see George."

"I'll take you to him, but you have to calm down. You're pale again. I need you to tell me you're okay."

"I just want to see George," I whined.

He blotted my face, and then handed me the hanky. "Blow your nose. And then I want you to take a deep breath."

I did what he asked.

Then he took me by the hand and we moved around the outside circle of the party.

It was a hot June day, and I sweated from every pore. I'm not a runner but nothing was going to keep me from my dog.

And that's when I saw him.

George was in a gated pen lying on the ground. There was something on his side, and he was licking it.

"What is that?"

My boyfriend cleared his throat. "It's a kitten," he said.

"Why is there a kitten on George? He doesn't like cats. I'm so confused."

"Let's sit down," Jake said.

"That's a good idea."

"Is Ainsley okay?" It was Shannon, but she stood in front of the sun, so I couldn't see her.

"I think she misunderstood me and ran all the way here.

She thought George was hurt."

"Not hurt," I said. "Kitten." My brain was fried. It was a combination of being tired and having way too much adrenaline in my system.

"I'm going to get you something to eat and drink," Shannon said.

"That's a good idea," Jake said.

"The good news is that thanks to George, the clinic has had a record number of adoptions at this party," Jake said. "There were about fifteen kittens in that pen. A few dogs, in another one. And several gerbils. Every animal has already been adopted, except for that kitten."

"Where are we?"

"It's the fundraiser for the free vet clinic, remember? I went to the shop to pick you up, but you weren't there. So I brought George here and decided we'd wait for you. George climbed in the pen with the kittens, and has been quite gentle with them. But I can't get him to leave. And he won't let anyone else take that last kitten. That's why I called you."

It was all beginning to make sense.

"Why does Ainsley look like she ran a marathon?" It was my brother.

"I think she did," Shannon said as she put a cup in my hand. "Drink this."

The cool water was like a blessing on my parched throat.

"Did you tell her about the kitten?" my brother asked.

"I was getting to it."

Then it hit me what he'd said. George had the kitten in his mouth.

I was about to scream at him, but then he stepped gently

over the gate, and brought the soggy kitten to me. He plopped it in my lap, and then did that weird thing where it looks like he's smiling.

"You can't have a kitten," I said. "I'm allergic."

George barked loudly. And everyone went silent. He'd never barked at me like that.

"He or she is your friend, but we can't take it home."

George moved closer and put his jaw on my shoulder. This was his idea of a hug. Then he backed away and nudged my hand so that it was on top of the kitten. I pet it, and it mewled at me. It was all black and had the most beautiful green eyes.

I scooped it up, and the kitten put a paw on my nose.

"Tell her the name of the cat," Greg whispered, as if trying not to destroy the moment.

"Julia Roberts," Jake said.

I started laughing, maybe somewhat hysterically, but they all joined on. The free clinic often named their animals after celebrities. That's how George ended up with his name. You're allowed to change it, but I made it official on his registration. It fit him. He was handsome, protective, and funny.

George cocked his head.

"Fine," I said. "We'll take your friend home. But we are not going to have the whole *Ocean's Eleven* cast staying at the house. Understood?"

"Ruh-ruh," George grumbled.

"Okay, I guess I'm adopting a kitten."

"Pushover," Greg said.

"Pay up," Shannon said. "I told you she'd do it. I

couldn't deny George either."

"Cats are great," Jake said. "Ains, I hate to do this to you, but my shift begins in ten minutes. Are you okay? I need you to say the words."

"Yes. I'm fine. I thought George was dead all the way over here."

George put his paw on my knee, as if to reassure me.

"I would do anything for you, silly dog. Including, adopting a kitten."

Jake kissed my forehead. "Do you have ride home?"

"I'll take her," Greg said.

My legs had started to cramp. I wasn't even sure I could stand up they hurt so bad. I hadn't run that fast or far in a really long time.

Jake rubbed his fingers across my cheek. It was a sweet gesture, but I wondered if he was trying to take my temperature. "They have a small crate and food for her, as part of the adoption package," he said.

He bent down and hugged George. "Congratulations, dude, on your new kitten. Be careful with her. She's super tiny."

George cocked his head, and then licked Jake's nose.

We all laughed.

After he left, Greg found one of vet techs at the clinic, who brought by a clipboard full of papers. "Normally, we make people wait forty-eight hours, before we complete the adoption, but since you are a repeat customer, we're going to let her go with you today."

"Thanks," I said.

"Well, I'm not sure George Clooney would have let her

stay another night. They are very attached. He's going to be a great substitute mom," the tech said.

"I have to admit, I don't know anything about caring for cats." Of course, when I'd adopted George at the same event years ago, I didn't know anything about Great Danes. I thought I'd go home with a much smaller dog, but he won my heart. Now, he was making me adopt a cat.

"Basically, you put food, water, and a litter box down for them, and that's it. They pretty much take care of themselves."

The kitten crawled up to nestle on my shoulder.

I sneezed, one hand holding the kitten so she didn't fall off and the other covering my mouth. "I think I'm allergic."

"She probably has some pollen in her fur," the tech said. "I'm kind of allergic but I use Flonase every day."

Great, and now I had to buy drugs. This was not how I saw this day going. Still, the purring in my ear was totally winning me over. That George so obviously adored her didn't hurt either.

By the time we loaded everything up in Greg's SUV, I was ready to go home and sleep for a few days.

"That might have been the cutest thing I've seen in a long time, but I still can't believe you adopted a cat."

George had insisted the kitten ride with him in the middle seat. He was stretched out and the kitten was curled up on his back.

"I was on my way to see you, when Jake called."

"What about?"

"Did Shannon tell you about Jere?"

"The guy who went with you guys last night?"

"Yeah. He had a tattoo that said *Bros*."

"Uh. Okay."

"The top of the B was that same serif font I saw on the guy who ran past me in the park."

Greg frowned. "Do you think he's our guy?"

I sighed. "I don't know him that well, but he really seemed to respect the victim. He got a tattoo representing him last night. And he's a nice guy."

"Is there motive?" Greg asked.

I'd half expected him to bite my head off for interfering. "None that I've seen so far. He says they were just friends but I wonder if there might have been a relationship there."

"What about all the money?" Greg asked.

"I was there when they found out about the inheritance. He and Lizzie were shocked. He could have been faking. I've been thinking about that but I don't know."

"Is that all you wanted to tell me?" he asked as he pulled up in my driveway.

"No. You always tell me I need to pay attention to the facts? I'm trying to do that but my gut is saying something really different."

"What do you mean?"

"I feel like the killer is right in front of our face. We have lots of motive, but how much opportunity? I'd like to take a look at the files."

Cue the yelling.

He pulled into my driveway and turned off his car.

Then he opened his door and got out.

"Are you going to sit there all night? Get your laptop and let's find our murderer."

Chapter Nineteen

THE NEXT MORNING I woke up with a kitten on my head and George snoring loudly at my feet. Greg and I had gone over all the details so many times there was little room left for anything else in my brain.

Luckily, we'd narrowed down our suspect list. There were those who were involved in the incident, and the family and coworkers. Lucy had done her due diligence by talking to most of the staff who worked with Mort.

Everyone said the same thing: He was the best boss they'd ever had. He insisted on excellence but he was fair and kind. All of his employees mentioned he made work fun and had a great sense of humor.

It didn't make sense for this guy to basically write the family out of his will. There were conflicting stories about the brothers, but it was all hearsay. No one had talked to Levi yet.

Greg left around midnight, but I'd stayed up another couple of hours going over everything one more time.

I lifted the kitten off my head, and sat her on the floor. She mewled.

George's eyes opened and he was on the floor faster than I'd ever seen him. He lifted Julia in his mouth and headed for the laundry room.

"What are you doing, dude?"

The door was open, and he put Julia in her litter box. She tried to crawl out, but he gently nudged her back. He did it several times, very patiently, until she did her business.

"You are the smartest dog in the world. How did you— Why ask? I shouldn't be surprised anymore."

After letting him out, I put food in their bowls and loved on the kitten while we waited for George. There were squirrels on the back fence, but he didn't care. He set a record on doing his thing and was at the back door in minutes.

"Maybe, we should have adopted a kitten years ago," I said.

An hour later, I parked in the back of the shop. I'd just set George and the kitten up in my office, when I received a text from Shannon.

Bakery now.

Yawning, I let Maria know I'd be back soon. It was a Friday, so we had plenty of staff. I'd basically come in to catch up on paperwork and make sure we were okay inventory-wise.

It was after nine, and the rush was over. There were only a couple of people in the bakery. One was Jere and the other was Levi. I recognized him from the funeral.

Lizzie had her arms crossed but she didn't appear angry.

"Tell her," Jere said. "Tell her what you said to me."

None of them seemed to realize I was there. I sat down at one of the tables by the window so I didn't disturb them.

"I—" Levi shook his head. "I'm glad you and Jere received the inheritance. Mom is—well, you can imagine.

Mort and I talked about it years ago. He told me what he'd planned and I knew it was coming."

That was a motive for murder.

He laughed. "Mom—I may not go home for a couple of days. Oh, it's not home anymore is it? Everything belongs to you."

For some reason, he didn't sound upset.

As fascinating as it was, my brain hurt. Rudely, I texted every word to Greg, as fast as my thumbs could type.

"I've always adored you, Lizzie. You were the best thing that ever happened to my brother. That's why he was so desperate to keep you in his life. All of this should have been yours."

Lizzie's lips were a thin line. Usually, she wore her heart on her sleeve, but I had no idea what she was thinking.

"I had to come see you in person. I don't want anything from you or Jere. I'd like to keep my job, but I understand if you need to replace me. I've alerted the police here that Mom is in a fit. I warned her to stay away but she doesn't listen."

Everyone stood there awkwardly for at least a minute.

"Thank you," Lizzie said. "This situation is uncomfortable for all of us. I've always liked you, Levi, for this reason. But your mother has tried to hurt me more than once. I imagine she'll be taking Jere and me to court soon."

Levi shook his head. "The will is iron-clad. Mom would be wasting her money. I told her as much. She might think about it, but it won't happen. I can't promise that but I think we are all ready to move on."

"I hope so. Jere and I need you at the company. We'll

have our hands full as it is. And, as a gesture of good faith, I'm giving the home back to you. If you want to live there, great, but sell it if you want.

"I have no desire to live there. My home is in Sweet River. I'm happy here with my friends, who already feel like family."

"You don't have to do that," he said.

"I want to. I belong here. This is home."

Lizzie uncrossed her arms. "Come give me a hug. I've missed you."

I slipped out the door.

Well, I guess that was another suspect I could cross off the list.

Maybe.

I had an idea. A way to discover why someone killed Mort.

I just had to convince everyone else involved.

Chapter Twenty

JASMINE HAD GONE all out for our special weekend. We'd stopped calling it a girls' weekend because we'd invited Jere. It was quite different than what we had planned a few days ago.

I parked my SUV and said a little prayer. As long as we all survived tonight, I was going to call this a win.

My brother thought I was nuts, but then he had to work within the parameters of the law.

My friends and I do not. Though, the only person who knew why we were doing this was Jasmine. Shannon had a hard time keeping a secret and if she had any clue what we hoped would happen, she'd be a nervous wreck.

Not that I wasn't. The nerves jangled hard in my stomach.

Carrie had to dog- and kitten-sit for me, so that I could focus on finding out information. Besides, her brothers were so excited to have a dog and a kitten around. I had a feeling poor George would be tired when I picked him up later.

Jasmine's old Southern mansion had been transformed into a dreamy house that might have sat right in the French Quarter. It was a Georgian style and had gone from haunted-house scary to something that could have been in *Architectural Digest*.

It's amazing how fast things can be done with an unlimited budget.

I knocked on the arched double doors.

"Hey," Jasmine said. "Come in."

"This place." I made a circle in her foyer.

"It's better than I imagined," Jasmine said. "There's still work to do on the third floor and the cellar is like something out of a horror film, but the rest is not bad."

I laughed. "You are consistently the Queen of Understatement. Is anyone else here?"

"No. You're the first and I'm glad. I need to go over a few things with you."

"Whatever you need." I followed her into the living area.

"Do you think there's a chance—" It was as if she couldn't say the words.

"We will be fine. I honestly think this was a crime of passion. Otherwise, the killer would have murdered Gran and Becky. Greg and Lucy will be nearby in the security room with your guards, and there will be two more deputies stationed outside your house."

She breathed deeply, and so did I. "I think I needed to tell myself that, as much as you had to hear it." We laughed.

"We got this. I do feel bad that Lizzie and Shannon aren't in on it," she said.

"Greg says it's need to know. Shannon gets nervous in these situations and Lizzie is an unknown factor—my brother's words. We are all grateful you are doing this and sharing your home."

"I'd do anything for you." We hugged.

"There's just been one small change," she said as she led

me to her gorgeous new living area. There were gardenias, hydrangeas, and roses everywhere. In the dining area there was a smorgasbord of food and a huge cake on a table in the corner. The furniture was elegant but simple, very much like the owner.

"It's all so beautiful," I said. I liked my house. It was a farmhouse and a very sort of put your feet up on the coffee table kind of place. But Jasmine's deserved a full-page spread in a magazine.

"I'd take all the credit, but I had some help from my designer friends in L.A. Thank goodness for video messaging. I'm not into fancy—you saw my condo in Houston—but this place needed something elevated. And that's my friend's word not mine. It's kind of New Orleans meets farmhouse and it feels like home for sure."

"That's the best part."

The doorbell rang.

She clapped her hands. "Places, people, the show is about to begin."

I laughed so hard I had to bend over.

"What's so funny?" Shannon asked. She was carrying a huge gift.

I frowned. "Who is that for?"

"You, silly. It's your birthday present. Duh. That's why we're here." She sat it down on the floor by the cake.

I'd forgotten that was the pretense for the party. My birthday was the next day, so it had made sense.

"But this is a housewarming gift for Jasmine." She handed it to our friend. It was wine in a velvet wine bag.

"The one thing you can never have too much of," Jasmine joked.

After pouring some wine, we sat down on the sofas while we waited for the others.

Thunder cracked overhead, and we all jumped a little.

I'd been so busy I hadn't checked the weather in days. Usually, in this part of Texas, it was super-hot and muggy, and would be for several weeks. The kind of hot where I get wet just going outside to my car.

The doorbell rang again. This time it was Levi and Jere. "We drove over together," he said. But he didn't look happy about it.

Did they have words in the car?

"Thank you for inviting me," Levi said. His face was a mask of politeness, but his eyes darted around the room. "Where's Lizzie?"

"She'll be here soon," Jasmine said. "She texted a few minutes ago and said she was running a little late. Some sort of late order at the bakery. You two come on in and let's get you some wine. Unless you prefer something stronger?"

"Wine is great," Levi said. The two men followed her to the bar.

But Jere stopped, came over and kissed my cheek and then Shannon's. "Hello, my best new girlfriends."

"Hi," we said.

"This is my—I mean, Levi," he said.

"It's great to meet you. Lizzie and Jere adore you all. They wouldn't stop talking about you."

He did seem like a nice guy.

After everyone picked up their wine, Jasmine made a toast. "To my bestie Ains, who has the biggest heart and is always there for her friends. Happy birthday, Ains."

The heat on my cheeks was burning. "Thank you. I'm glad we all had time to get together," I said. "And it's fun to have new friends." I raised my glass to the men.

The doorbell rang. It was a very frazzled Lizzie. When she finally sat down with a glass of wine, she took a deep breath. Then she patted my hand. "Sorry I'm late," she said. "It was a little crazy late this afternoon."

"No worries. We still have *some* wine left."

Everyone laughed and relaxed in their chairs.

"We are grown-ups," Jasmine said. "But I have all these icebreaker games from years of working with corporate folks. It's a great way to get to know people fast. And you don't have to answer anything that might make you feel uncomfortable."

"Oh, I love a good game." Jere clapped his hands like a child who'd just been given some candy.

"First question is a serious one." Jasmine smiled. "The zombie apocalypse is nigh. What three people are on your team?"

Everyone's answers were really funny. I picked Shannon, Jasmine, and Lizzie. I didn't like leaving the new guys out, but it was the zombie apocalypse; one must choose wisely. "Shannon makes the coffee, Lizzie makes the cake, and Jasmine can make anything happen in minutes." We all laughed.

"It's good to have your priorities: coffee and cake, and a wizard," Levi said.

"Exactly," I said.

"Okay." Jasmine pulled out a new card. "Where did you

go on your last date and who was it with?"

"Does the night we all went out count?" Lizzie asked. "I can't even remember the last time I went out on a date."

"Honey, that's just sad. We need to do something about that," Jere said.

"My last date was with…Kane, and we went for a picnic by the lake. It was nearly perfect right up until the mosquitos came out and we ran into some fire ants. I'm still itchy." Jasmine rubbed her arms.

"Whoo-hoo," I said under my breath. I loved that she and Kane were dating.

"Don't get any ideas, Ains. We're taking it slow."

I stared up at the ceiling. "I have no idea what you're talking about. And my last date was with Jake. We had pizza and doughnuts and watched *My Fair Lady*. He didn't even complain that it was a musical."

"Because it's like the best musical ever," Shannon said.

Jere raised his glass to that. "Audrey gets me every time."

"Me too," Jasmine said. "How about you, Shannon?"

"Well, since I got married, I only get to date my husband. It's a rule or something," she joked. "But it's busy wine season. He's exhausted, and I fall asleep at eight most nights. But we've been watching *Luther*, which we love. I decided that my next husband would be Idris Elba. Mike said that was fine, as long as he could hang out with us. I think he has a man crush."

"Hear. Hear," Jere said. "We will all drink to that."

"Okay, Jere. So, who was your last date?" I asked.

He stared down at his shoes uncomfortably. Then he glanced at Levi and they held eyes.

Wait. What?

"Are you two dating?" Shannon asked. "That's so cool. Why didn't you tell us?"

Levi cleared his throat. "I'm not out yet," he said. "We're being discreet, especially now with everything that's going on at the company."

"Your secret is safe with us," Shannon said. "I am sorry you don't feel like you can be yourself in public, but you're in a safe circle. Or maybe we should be a coven. I've always loved witches."

"Me, too," Jere said. "I have to show you the witch's hat on my knee. That one hurt, but it was worth it."

"I'm so glad you felt comfortable enough to tell us," Jasmine said. "About the relationship."

Levi smiled tightly, and Jere reached out for his hand.

Then something clicked in my brain. "Did Mort know?" Crap. I hadn't meant to say that out loud.

They jumped.

"Sorry. It doesn't matter," I said. "Did I mention I have foot-in-mouth disease? I didn't mean to pry."

Shannon rolled her eyes. "It's a part of her nature. You get used to the inquisitions."

Good save, Shannon.

"But we love you," Jasmine said. "We'll do some more questions later, but now let's eat. I can't believe I didn't say that first."

There was a bit of a break as we were all chitchatting and filling our plates. The awkwardness was gone.

"My brother did know," Levi said from beside me. I nearly dropped my plate because I hadn't seen him move.

"Oh. I hope he was happy for you," I said.

He frowned. "I wouldn't say that. I feel sorry for Jere, because he's been caught in the middle of all of this. It's not fair to him but I can't let him go."

The love in his voice was evident. I thought I knew who the killer was, but maybe I'd been wrong.

"It feels a bit like throwing stones at glass houses," I said.

"Right? It's complicated. We have rules at work and they are there for a reason."

Jere and Lizzie were having an intense conversation in the huge kitchen.

I wonder what that's about?

"Those two are hilarious. They're probably fighting over Superman and Batman." He laughed but it wasn't a happy sound.

Before I could head that way, Jasmine called to me.

"Greg wants you to keep your phone on you," she whispered. "He has a couple of questions he wants you to squeeze into the conversation."

"Yeah, because I haven't made things awkward enough tonight. This is why I don't do parties."

We laughed.

Another crack of thunder made everyone jump.

"This is why I moved the party indoors," Jasmine said. "Besides, until the pool and patio area screened in, I'm not going outside at night again. It's going to be like this for a few hours, so let's ignore it and have some fun. If the power goes out, I have quite a few generators, so we'll be fine," she said to the group.

The weather must have been the big change she'd been

talking about. Good news for me. I wouldn't have to lie and say I forgot my swimsuit. I'm not a big party person and pool parties are the worst. It probably wasn't such a big deal for Jasmine, who looked like Halle Berry. But me—nope.

Rain poured down and we stared out at the pool area she'd mentioned.

"That's a lot of rain," Levi said.

"My dad would call this a gully washer," Shannon said.

"I've never heard that," Lizzie said. "I'm not sure I know what a gully is. I'm guessing some sort of ravine where water runs."

Shannon shrugged. "I think so but when we were kids, it meant the street would flood, so we could sail boats to the end of the block. That was of course before we worried about things like typhoid and a thousand other diseases you can get from flood waters."

I chuckled. "Funny, for kids the whole world is a wonderland of fun. And then grown-ups are afraid of everything."

"Well, some of us are more fun than others," Jere said snottily. He was in some sort of mood and he wouldn't stop glaring at Lizzie. Whatever had happened put a new rift between the friends.

Was she upset he was dating Levi and didn't tell us? I completely understood why they wouldn't. One thing I did know about her was that she was fair and kind to everyone she met. People said that about me, but they had no idea how judgey I could be sometimes. But Lizzie wasn't like that.

"Lizzie, did you try these canapés Shannon brought? I could eat the whole plate." She followed me over.

"Is everything okay?" I whispered.

Her brows drew together. "What do you mean?"

"The fighting?"

She sighed. There was a lot of that going on these days.

"He should have told me about Levi. We've been talking about all this business stuff and making it a smooth transition. What if the board finds out they are dating? I don't want them to stop, but I can't protect Levi and Jere's jobs, if they aren't honest with me."

She cared so much about people.

"I don't think they meant to be secretive, as much as protective of Levi."

She pressed her lips together. "I understand that now. But I had to ask him if they were hiding anything else. Then he acted a little fishy, and wouldn't tell me anything. I'm not mad—more annoyed."

What were they hiding?

Then two things happened at once. The lights went out and someone banged hard on the door.

My body tensed, and there was a scream. This time it wasn't from me.

I had a feeling Depends would be a part of my future wardrobe if this continued.

Chapter Twenty-One

I MANEUVERED THROUGH the dark and met Jasmine at the door. Someone hit the door hard, and we grabbed each other. She tried to show me her phone, but it was a black screen.

"The security system is temporarily out," she whispered, as she glanced at her phone. "But the generators should kick in soon."

She peeped through the small hole in one of the doors, and then glanced back at me and frowned.

"Who is it?"

"You'll see."

She opened the door and in walked a very wet Jake and Mike, and just behind them were my brother and Lucy. Then Kane ran up.

"Is everything okay?" I asked.

"Yeah," Jake said. "We wanted to surprise you." He hugged me. "Just play along," he whispered.

"Sorry we were late," Lucy said, and then hugged me like an old friend. She and I got along better than when we first met, but we weren't that friendly. That sounds mean. But I'd never seen Lucy hug anyone.

My brother hugged me, which never happened. "Follow my lead. It will all make sense soon."

They all had presents. "Those go by the cake." Jasmine pointed toward the dining room. "Grab some food and wine, and we'll get started on the next game."

She was better at playing along than I was. One of the suspects must have said something that had him call in the troops. But the for the life of me, I had no idea what it was. My brain was still trying to figure things out when fingers snapped in front of my face.

I focused and found Jake smiling at me. "We really did surprise you."

I nodded and then grinned at him. "Best surprise ever," I said louder than necessary.

There was a strange buzzing and the lights popped back on.

Everyone laughed and then introductions were made. It could have been any party anywhere, except one person was possibly the killer.

"Everyone load up your plates and we'll start the next game."

༄

A FEW MINUTES later, we sat in a large circle. "Jasmine, is it okay if we play my favorite game?"

"Yes. I have the papers you asked for ready."

"What game is it?" Jake asked.

"Werewolf assassin," I said. "It's like the game Mafia you probably played when you were a kid, except, I like werewolves better. Do you guys know how to play?"

"It's been so long," Shannon said. "I think maybe I was

in collage the last time."

"I've never heard of it," Lizzie said.

"We used to play it at family gatherings. It can get pretty heated." He smiled. "Maybe it will be better with strangers.

"It's a fun way to find out what people are really like," Greg added. "Birthday girl used to make me and my friends play all the time."

"You liked it and so did your friends." I smirked.

I gave a quick explanation. "It sounds complicated but it's easier once we get going. The important thing is to try and fool everyone and to never reveal your identity until it's time. And don't take it personally, especially for those of you who are new to our little group. It's all in good fun. And remember, if you're a werewolf, it's important to lie as well as possible, and pretend to be a human."

I handed out the pieces of paper, and I cheated. I knew who was getting what role. The narrator, detectives, and werewolves were all carefully designed before we arrived. Though, now we had a few more people than I'd been expecting.

The great thing about the game is I would be able to see who was gifted at lying.

We began, and I told the werewolves to open their eyes and see who was on their team. Their job was to band together and make it seem like one of the civilians were the assassin. I asked the detective, who was Lucy, to ask her first question.

"How many people have you killed?" she asked.

It was interesting to listen to the responses from each of the werewolves and I watched carefully to see who the best liar was. Two of them had tells, though they probably had no idea.

The third was slick and very good at lying. Interesting. That was unexpected. Did I have it all wrong?

We came to the part where the civilians had to vote one person out of the game. It was all I could do not to laugh out loud when Jasmine was voted out. She was supposed to stay in until the last two, but she wasn't a very good liar. The whole gist of it was the best liar would be left standing.

By the end of the game, there were three people left and I was more confused than ever.

Greg glanced at me and frowned. He too, was surprised by the outcome. He had to be wondering the same thing. Did we get it all wrong?

Our party had taken an interesting turn. My mind whirled with possibilities when it came to the game we just finished. Everyone stared in shock as Lizzie laughed hysterically. "I can't believe I won. I never win games."

None of this made sense. Lizzie had been with Shannon and Jasmine when the murder happened. Besides she was five foot and I'd be surprised if she weighed a hundred pounds soaking wet. She was the epitome of petite, which wasn't fair since she made delicious cakes and cookies all day.

A few people stood up and stretched.

"What is going on?" Shannon mouthed. "I feel like I just missed something major."

"Later," I whispered back.

"Hey, Lizzie, congrats on your win," Lucy said. "You probably don't want to talk business tonight, but I need to make an appointment. I promised my sister I'd get a unicorn cake from you for my niece."

Lizzie smiled sweetly. "I'm always happy to talk about cake." They went off toward the food.

Lucy had separated her from the pack for a reason.

I glared at Greg and shook my head.

There was no way Lizzie was guilty.

Levi and Jere were getting themselves more wine. Greg and I jumped up and motioned to Kane to meet us by the front door.

"What's up?"

"How sure is the time of death?" I asked.

He glanced at Greg.

"I want to know the same thing," Greg answered.

"You guys understand that it's always approximate. There is no way to know exactly when it happened. But not much rigor had set in. I'd say from the time the body was found, it was within an hour and a half, maybe."

My stomach churned.

"And you are sure it had to be a man?"

He shrugged. "Or a tall and strong woman. Very strong."

A pain struck the back of my eyeball. I rubbed my eye.

"I think you just broke Ainsley's brain," Greg joked.

"Why all the questions?" Kane asked. "We've talked about this a couple of times."

I sighed.

"Lizzie is a more adept liar than we could have ever imagined," Greg whispered.

"Yes, or no one thought it could be her because she's so sweet and has an air of innocence about her," Kane said.

"But there's no way she had the physical strength to do that kind of damage."

"She has guilt about that night," Greg said. "She might be an accomplice or an innocent bystander. That's what Lucy is doing right now. Without asking about that night, just about her history and such. We can't find much about her background."

"She went to school with the victim. They married way too young. He came out and they got divorced. And then they ended up as friends. She's been spending time all over America studying different baking styles. What else do you need to know?"

Kane laughed. "Maybe you should just hire Ainsley as a full-time consultant."

"Don't give her any ideas."

Jere and Levi held hands and were adorable together. I just didn't see them as killers.

But who could it be?

Pictures flashed through my brain and they moved so fast that I could barely keep up. And then one face was left. That had never happened before but it was like my subconscious had known who the killer was all along.

"Oh. No."

"What is it?" Greg asked.

"Lizzie may know more than what she and Becky have said. I want a chance to talk to her alone first. Okay?"

Greg appeared puzzled for a moment, and then it was as if a lightbulb had gone off. Before he could say anything, Lizzie walked up. "I feel like you guys are talking about me," she said, and she didn't look happy about it.

I took her hands in mine. "I think it's time you tell us everything."

Her shoulders slumped. "I can't. I made a promise."

"I know you think you are protecting her, but that kind of trauma could cause permanent damage. She needs help. Serious, psychological help."

Her eyes watered and she shook her head. "I thought I was doing the right thing, but I don't know anymore."

She went and sat down in a big fluffy chair in the living room. Her head in her hands, she waited.

Everyone gathered around and I knelt by her chair and took her hand. "It's okay. You had the very best intentions. We all know that. Take your time and tell us everything."

"What's going on?" Jere asked. "Why is Lizzie crying?"

Shannon shushed him.

"Why don't we take a seat," Lucy said. At least everyone wouldn't be looming over her.

Greg turned on the recorder on his phone, and then sat down in the chair next to Lucy.

Shannon leaned forward and handed Lizzie some tissues.

"That night, I'd run out to get more sugar before I headed over here. Business had been much better than I'd planned and we'd gone through so much. I bought all they had at the grocery store."

"Did you go back to the bakery?"

"No. I told her I would, but I didn't. I was running late to come here, so I texted her to just finish up and head home. I left her there alone." She sobbed. "She texted back that she was scared. I told her she'd be fine and to lock the door when she left."

She took a deep shuddering breath.

"When I found out about the murder—I didn't know what to think. I had a suspicion that he'd surprised her. He had a habit of trying to scare the wits out of people. He thought it was a funny joke."

"I can attest to that," Jere said.

"So can I," Levi added. He didn't seem as upset as I would have expected. Maybe he just wanted to know what happened as much as the rest of us did.

"What you don't know, is she and another girl were mugged on a school trip. The men who did it made them get on their knees execution-style, and then shot off their gun. Both girls were traumatized. And that just happened last year. It's why she wanted to move away from home. Everyone looked at her with pity.

"Loud noises bother her, and she's afraid of men. She told me about it when we first met. In the beginning, I thought they'd all been attacked. But then some of the facts started to come out about the suspect being tall and strong."

Suspects usually tried to throw shade at one another. Lizzie didn't seem the type to do that. Was she making it look like Becky did it?

"She's not small and used to do shot put in high school. But she makes the most delicate flowers for cakes you've ever seen.

"The day after everything happened, she called me but she couldn't remember anything. I promised her that I would take care of everything but she was in a daze. She kept saying, 'He touched me. He touched me.'"

She coughed and then put the tissues to her nose. "She

whispered it and I asked her who touched her. When a young girl says that, your mind goes to the worst places. Then she said: the man. The man at the bakery. He'd probably surprised her and she panicked. I had to protect her.

"All of this is my fault. If I'd done what I promised. He'd still be alive, and Becky wouldn't be suffering so much."

"Did she tell you anything about that night?" Greg asked.

"Nothing past what I told you, and what she explained to you guys. It's still not clear in her head. I honestly don't know how Mrs. Whedon ended up in there. I'm sorry, Ainsley. I had to protect her, like I would any friend. And I wasn't sure what exactly she'd done. I don't think I was aware at the time how messed up it was. I may have said to her that her memories were probably all mixed up. And that we'd ask Ainsley to help sort things. But I told her until the memories came back, that she should keep quiet."

Her hands were shaking so hard, that I held them in mine.

"Hey, you're in a safe space. Do you think Becky killed Mort?"

She trembled. "You have to understand that I didn't even process everything that had happened, and my part in it, until the funeral. I thought it best if everyone thought it was just a random person. Maybe a robbery. I'd planned to tell Ainsley on the way home after the funeral that I might have an idea of what happened. But I'd just found out that I'd inherited part of the company.

"I didn't see it happen, but she was the only one there.

There's no way Mrs. Whedon did it. Becky can't remember much except that someone touched her and then she was in the freezer. I'm sorry to all of you. This is not who I am but I was so scared for her."

"Becky is adorable," Shannon said. "I honestly might have done the same thing."

We all turned to look at her.

"If it were one of you, I'd do anything to protect you. Are you saying you wouldn't do the same?" She pointed to me and Jasmine. "We made a pact to bring a shovel if anyone of us called. No questions asked."

She was right. We had made that pact when Jasmine had been going through all of her family stuff. There wasn't anything I wouldn't do for them.

"I think maybe I shouldn't be hearing this," Greg said. He said it in a way that made me snort. Shannon, Jasmine, and I laughed hysterically while the rest of the room just stared at us.

"Sorry," I said, as I tried to pull myself together. "I laugh when I'm stressed. So do Shannon and Jasmine. It's one of the reasons we're friends. Inappropriate laughing. We're usually the worst at funerals."

Lizzie reached out and hugged me. "I'm so sorry about everything, and especially Mrs. Whedon. You have to understand I would never do anything to put her in danger."

I hugged her back. "I have a feeling she did that all by herself."

"Promise me you'll come visit me in prison?" she asked.

"You're not going to prison," I said.

"She did aid and abet a murder suspect," Lucy chimed

in. She was always so helpful when it came to the law.

"Did she?" I asked. "She suspected Becky might have killed Mort, but she had no proof. And how did Mrs. Whedon end up in the freezer? Would any of us have turned Becky in if we heard this same story a few weeks ago?"

Jake shook his head. His hand had been on my back this whole time, giving me strength.

"We would have done exactly what we've been doing," I said. "I mean, we might have tried to get her some psychological help."

"Ains makes a fair point," Greg said. "We would have badgered Becky for the truth, and might have done more harm than good to her mental state."

Lucy rolled her eyes. "Greg, you've gone soft." But there was no harshness in her tone.

He shook his head. "I keep reminding you that this is a small town and we look out for our own."

She sighed and looked hurt.

Hmmm. There might have been trouble in paradise but there was no time to solve that mystery now.

"Becky. We need to get to her or at least warn her parents," I said. "If she starts to remember—I don't know what will happen."

Greg's phone buzzed. He scowled at the message.

"What is it?" Lucy asked.

"Becky's missing."

Chapter Twenty-Two

A HALF HOUR later we were in Becky's parents' barn in Round Top. We'd picked up George but left Julia Roberts with Carrie. My dog is great at finding people—not just dead ones.

Jake's search and rescue team had joined the one in Round Top and there were at least forty other people there willing to go out and look for her in the torrential rains. They'd loaned all of us raincoats and hats, and big boots that didn't fit.

One of the guys from the rescue whistled sharply and everyone quieted down. "We've assessed the situation. It's dangerous out there. The ground was dry so the flooding is worse than usual. For now, until it stops, Chief Jake from Sweet River has helped us formulate a plan and it's a good one. So, listen up."

Jake cleared his throat. "We have a young and possibly frightened girl out there."

He was interrupted by several gasps.

"What's wrong?" Shannon whispered.

We were on the far side of the barn, and couldn't see what was coming in.

"It's Becky's horse," her mom cried.

Oh. No. That couldn't be good. *Please, don't let anything*

happen to her. I sent up a silent prayer. She might be a murderer but poor Becky had been through enough.

Some police officers took the mother back to the house.

"Right," Jake said. "We've broken the ranch into quadrants. It's important that the teams stay together. It's easy to miss things in weather like this. You're looking for clothing, or tracks, if there are any left. And anything that might be out of place. We check in every fifteen minutes. I can't stress this enough: do not try to be a hero. The last thing we need right now is to have to save someone else."

He sounded so authoritative and strong. My heart did double time.

Get it together, Ainsley. This is no time to daydream about Jake.

"When I call your names, please come forward."

He broke everyone up into teams of five.

Jasmine, Shannon, me, Jere and Levi, were the last five.

"I need you guys to search her room and around the barn. Try to find us some sort of clue to where she's gone. This is a big ranch, and we have too much ground to cover with this kind of weather."

"We can go out searching with you," I said. "This isn't some sort of design to keep me safe."

He smirked. "You are better at finding clues than any detective I've ever met. Look for photos, anything that might give us some idea where she is. This is going to be hard enough in the rain and with it pitch-black. Find us something, please."

We all nodded.

"It's sweet that you guys came with us," Jasmine said. "I

would have thought you would have been really angry with Lizzie and Becky."

The two men looked at each other. "Tell them," Jere said.

Levi cringed. "I followed my brother that night," he whispered.

"What?" I asked.

"He was in such a mood when he found out about Jere and me. He had this hard and fast rule about not dating employees. Jere and I had been really discreet, but he must have seen us somewhere."

We needed to be searching for clues, but maybe Levi had seen something that night.

"Tell us everything," Shannon said. She didn't have kids yet, but she had that mom voice down.

"He didn't even know—none of my family does. He didn't care about that, but he was worried that we wouldn't be professional at the office. We had been for months, but he wouldn't listen. He was in one of these moods where he refuses to hear the other person."

"Okay," I said. "But how did you end up in Sweet River?"

"He'd mentioned he was coming here to see Lizzie. She—well, she's always been good to me. Even after everything that happened. I thought she might be able to make him see reason. He was going to fire Jere if we didn't stop dating."

Hmmm. Well, if that wasn't motive, I'm not sure what was.

"So it was you I saw in the park that night?"

He jumped back. "You saw me?"

"You ran past me and my dog."

"That was you?"

I nodded. "So, did you see the murder scene?"

He shook his head. "No. I heard people screaming. I thought it was Lizzie and my brother. They were friends but she would let him have it if he made her angry. I didn't want them to see me, so I ran off."

He hung his head. "If I hadn't been such a coward that night, my brother might still be alive. I just didn't want to make him angrier at me. I didn't see anything. They were yelling pretty loud. I was about twenty feet from the building."

"Think about what you actually heard," I said. "Just close your eyes and put yourself right outside of the building. What do you hear?"

He closed his eyes. The rain outside pounded the ground. I wasn't looking forward to making the small trek to the house. And our poor guys were out there in the thick of it.

"It's a woman's voice but I don't think it's Lizzie. She's screaming at him. How dare you. How dare you. And then he said something corny, like don't get your panties in a wad, woman. I would have been surprised if Lizzie hadn't killed him at that point, but I really don't think it was her."

Could that have been Mrs. Whedon? Maybe she'd stumbled upon the scene.

"I just ran off. I'm a coward and because of that, my brother is dead."

Jasmine hugged him from behind. "You don't know,"

she said. "Like with Lizzie, you didn't see anything. There's a chance you might have been hurt, as well."

I felt sorry for poor Lizzie. They wouldn't let her come try to find Becky. Greg said from here on out that they had to follow protocol. She was home with one of the officers waiting for our call.

"She's right. Let's get to the house and see if we can find something that will help the search and rescue gang," I said.

"We can search outside the house," Jere offered. "This is serious, but I did always win at hide-and-seek. Maybe, she's in one of the outbuildings we saw on our way in."

"If you guys are sure you don't mind."

"No problem," Levi said.

We headed into the house. Luckily, the rain softened a bit so it wasn't pelting so hard it hurt my skin. It was hot and muggy, especially in the raincoats.

As soon, as we were inside, I took mine off, and hung it on the rack by the door. A bunch of towels and mats had been put down to soak up moisture. I stepped out of the wet boots, and then onto the towels.

Becky's mom had calmed down and was seated at the table with another woman. It didn't feel right just barging into their house.

"Hi," I said. "I'm Ainsley McGregor and these are my friends. We all adore Becky. My brother, the sheriff from Sweet River, has asked us to go through her room and see if there are any clues as to where she might have gone."

The mom started to get up, but I waved her down. "Please, don't get up. We can find our way if you just point us in the right direction."

"It's the third door on the left," she said hoarsely. I couldn't imagine what it might be like to have a child who was missing. Well, Becky was a grown-up, but I had a feeling that didn't change no matter how old the kid was.

The house was large, and Becky's room very much looked like her. It was cheerful in bright yellows and pinks. There were photos everywhere and flowers. It was a happy place for a young girl.

I remembered being her age and wanting to paint my room black. My mom settled on a light blue.

Some of the pictures were with her friends, many of whom I'd seen in the barn. On her desk were a stack of photos. One was of her with her horse at the edge of a stream. Becky was beautiful with her long dark hair blowing in the wind and the sweetest smile. It was easy to see she was in her happy place.

"Oh," I said.

"What did you find?" Shannon asked. She and Jasmine walked over to me and I showed them the picture.

"She's gorgeous in this. I wonder if it was her senior picture?"

I walked back to the kitchen and showed the photo to her mom.

"Is this on the ranch?"

She took the picture and stared at it lovingly. "My beautiful girl," she whispered.

Her friend patted her hand. "Honey, they need to know where it was taken."

"By the creek over by the mesa," she said.

I had no idea where that was, but I grabbed the walkie-talkie that Jasmine had been given and headed back to Becky's room.

"Jake, Greg, are one of you there?"

"What did you find?" Greg asked.

"A photo of her by a stream. Her mom said it's near a mesa."

"Makes sense," Jake said. "George took off in that direction and I can't keep up with him, but he's barking and he's near. I'll let you know what we find."

Then they were radio silent for what seemed like forever.

"Please, God, let her be safe," Shannon said.

Jasmine and I bowed our heads. We all wanted the same thing. For that sweet girl to be okay.

"Lucy, call everyone in. Jake has eyes on her. He needs some help and I'm headed that way."

My heart, which already felt like it was going to jump out of my chest, beat even faster. Were Jake and George in danger?

They were in the middle of it and I knew better than to distract them.

That didn't keep the bile from burning my throat, and the tears from falling.

"They are fine," Shannon said. "Mike is with him and a lot of his guys. They probably just need some extra hands."

We headed back to the kitchen. I wasn't sure if her mom had heard, but it hit me that they didn't say anything about Becky being alive or fine. The last thing I wanted to do was distress her more.

I cleared my throat. "We're going to head out to the barn," I said. "I'm sure we'll hear something soon."

We put our raincoats back on. A few of the groups had already returned.

An ambulance pulled up with the lights flashing, and I took that as a good sign. It wasn't Kane's coroner van, which was already here. Unless—nope, I would not allow myself to imagine that Jake, George, or my brother might have been hurt.

The high-pitched whine of ATVs and a flash of lights hit just outside the barn door. We ran over to see what was going on. The EMTs jumped out with a stretcher. And several men carried Becky, who was covered head to toe in blankets on to the gurney. She was ghastly pale, and her eyes were shut.

Lucy had her arm around the mother and guided her into the ambulance, once they had the gurney set. The EMTs and Kane were busy working on her. And the mom hugged a man who was in the ambulance crying. I guessed that was Becky's dad. He was covered in dirt and brush.

"Let's go," Kane said.

The ambulance left, and everyone was left standing there wondering what happened.

"She's alive," someone said, who had come in with the team. "But she was in the water a long time. That dog saved her life."

George? Was he okay? And where were Jake and my brother?

My eyes burned with tears and as if they knew exactly what was happening, my two besties put hands on my shoulders and guided me to a hay bale.

Lucy walked over.

"Where are they?" Shannon asked.

I had the biggest lump in my throat and was grateful my friend had my back.

"They're coming," she said. "They had to wait for the ATV with the trailer."

"Lucy what happened?"

She knelt down. "George saved that girl's life," she said. And then she sniffed.

My heart fell to my stomach.

"She was in the middle of a river, which used to be a stream, and it was coming so fast. Rocks were pushed up from the ground. The limb holding Becky above the water broke, and George—"

I sobbed. *No. Please. Do. Not. Say. The words.*

"Ainsley, he was in that water a long time and used every bit of his strength to keep her head above the water. I've never seen such a heroic rescue. They hit a rock and he still held on but—"

My brave George. Shannon put her arms around me and I sobbed.

Just then there was a big commotion and another ambulance arrived.

I pushed my friend away and ran out. My brother drove an ATV with a trailer hitched to it. George and Jake were lying on it and neither of them moved.

"No!" I screamed.

Jake's eyes opened. "Ains?"

"Are you okay?"

"Broke my arm and maybe my ankle," he gritted out. He was soaking wet and covered in mud. But he was alive.

"It's George I'm worried about. He hit a rock hard, and he's taken in a lot of water. I'm sorry Ains, I couldn't stop him. He was determined to save her."

I put a hand on George, who struggled to breathe. "Oh, my sweet boy," I sobbed. "Jake said no heroes and look at the both of you."

"Get up," my brother ordered. "We need to get them to the hospital."

Men stood there with gurneys for both of them.

They were quickly loaded into the ambulance.

"Well are you coming?" My brother held out his hand.

Chapter Twenty-Three

"Ainsley," Jake whispered. "Hon, you need to wake up." I tried to force my eyes open but it was impossible.

"Tired," I said.

"I can imagine. You slept on a steel table."

Wait. Jake. My eyes popped open. He stood next to me with one arm in a cast and the other holding a crutch.

"Oh." I sat up fast and wrapped my arms around his neck. "Are you okay? Greg said you were, but I've been worried sick."

"I'm doing better than George." He frowned.

I glanced down at the pallet the vet and his tech had made in the corner of the room. George was asleep and bandaged from head to toe, wearing a cone of shame. He was too big to be comfortable in any of the kennels the vet had on hand, so they set us up in one of the vet check rooms.

"He's alive," I said. "That's all that matters."

Jake hugged me.

"I feel so guilty for not being at the hospital with you," I said. And it was true. He'd forced the ambulance driver to go to the vet hospital first and told me to go with George. That he would be fine. If George hadn't whined just then, I'm not sure I would have done what Jake wanted.

"Don't. I needed you here with our guy. I've been worried sick about him. He was so brave, Ainsley. Like, didn't take a moment's thought, just did what he had to in order to save Becky's life. I've trained with search and rescue dogs who wouldn't have been that fast or brave."

"And he almost killed himself and you. Greg told me what you did."

He shrugged and gave me that sly grin of his. "I was not going to let him die," I said.

The team had made a human chain to grab Becky and George with Jake and my brother in the water, pulling them to safety. But once George let go, a fast current ripped him out of Jake's hand. Jake let go of my brother, and floated down until he caught George.

When the guys tried to pull him in with the rope they'd yanked a little too hard and had pulled his shoulder out of the socket and had broken his wrists.

"Was your ankle broken?"

He shook his head. "Just swollen. I don't even remember hitting it. Everything happened so fast."

Jake helped me off the table with his good arm, and I knelt beside George. The doctors said he wasn't out of the woods yet. One of his ribs had been broken, and his skin rubbed raw in several places. That was why he was wrapped in gauze. They put a special ointment on his whole body to help him heal. And there'd been damage to some of his paws. They thought, because he was trying to get traction on the sharp rocks.

"Is Becky okay?" I asked. I sat on the floor and scratched George's ears. It was the only part of him that wasn't bandaged.

He tried to lift his head but he was still heavily sedated. The vet wanted to keep him still for twenty-four hours to give his rib time to set.

"It's okay, boy. You rest."

"She hasn't regained consciousness yet, but her vital signs are looking good. Her mother and father wanted to thank you and George for helping to save her life. If you hadn't told us where to look when you did, she would have drowned."

"George knew. Didn't he?"

Jake nodded. "He was definitely headed in that direction. I'm telling you, Ainsley, I've seen him run fast in the backyard and do his crazy thing, but never like that. It was as if he understood the gravity of the situation before we ever caught up with him. He was already leaping into the water when we got to the scene. I tried to catch him but I missed him."

"It's okay, Jake. I know you feel guilty but you saved his life, too."

George grunted.

"I think that means he's grateful," I said.

We both laughed.

"Any change with Gran?"

He shook his head. "Her vitals have improved and almost all the swelling is gone from her brain. The doctors think she might wake up any minute but said it's hard to predict exactly when."

Wake up, Gran. You're the only one who can tell us what really happened and possibly save Becky and Lizzie from prison.

Chapter Twenty-Four

A WEEK LATER, the Fourth of July parade was in full swing. Lizzie, who rented Shannon's apartment, had invited us to watch from the rooftop patio. We'd had a lot of parties up here when Shannon was living there, but this was the first one Lizzie had thrown.

She'd been cleared of any wrongdoing and I think she was just now beginning to feel somewhat normal. Her happy smile still hadn't come back, but like most of us, she probably needed a little time.

"There it is," Shannon squealed. "Look at George and Jake. They look so handsome."

Jake sat on a chair with George by his feet. I'd nixed the idea of George riding alone, and Jake offered to sit with him.

"And here come our heroes Fire Chief Jake and the town celebrity, and everyone's favorite Great Dane, Geooooorge Clooney," the announcer said.

The crowd went wild. Kids and adults jumped up and down yelling, "George. George. George."

I swear my dog sat up a little straighter. Being who he was, he'd healed quicker than anyone had expected. Even though it had only been a week. A tear dropped down my cheek as I watched my guys go by. Julia Roberts mewed in my hands.

"Yep, your big brother is putting on quite the show," I said.

"George's head is not going to be able to fit through your doors at home," Mike joked.

"You aren't wrong." I laughed.

After our float, came Shannon's. It was a giant smiling coffee cup that waved.

"Oh, Mike, it looks so good," she said. "Thank you."

"That's ingenuity," I said. "It looks like a real arm."

Mike laughed. "It is. We couldn't get the mechanism to work at the last minute so one of my guys took all the mechanical stuff out of the giant cup. His arms are completely covered in a blue sweater and matching gloves, so that it looks like the cup is waving. Wearing a sweater in July is hazardous. I have to pay him overtime but it's worth it."

"Thank you, honey. It pays to be married to a man who thinks fast on his feet."

"I thought I'd find you kids up here. Put me down, Judge."

That voice. I turned to find Gran in the arms of the judge. He was at least eighty. Had he carried her up the two flights of stairs?

"She is supposed to be in the hospital," he said. "But she demanded we come find you."

She put a hand on his chest. "Henry, put me down."

A look passed between them that was so sweet. He'd been by her bedside more often than not the last week.

I ran to them and kissed her cheek. "You're awake."

"Darn straight. Can't believe I was out for so long. But I was having the best dreams."

"Here, let me help you," Mike said as he tried to take her from the judge's arms.

"I'm all right, son. She weighs about as much as a sack of potatoes."

"Put me in that chair," she said, as she pointed to a lounger.

Shannon, Lizzie, and I sat down with her.

"Do you know where your brother is?"

I shook my head. "He was supposed to be here but he hasn't showed up yet."

"I need you to find him. There's something he needs to know and I don't have the energy to tell this story more than once tonight."

I pulled out my phone and texted my brother 911. We'd promised only to use it for emergencies. That way he'd know it was important.

"I'm here," he said. He must have been coming up the stairs. "What's—Gran, what are you doing here?"

"Come here, boy. I have something to tell you."

She leaned back on the lounger as everyone gathered around her.

"Turn your recorder on—you're gonna need this."

She patted Lizzie's hand. "I'm glad to see you, hon. Are you okay?"

"Yes, ma'am."

"We're just happy you're awake," Shannon said. "How are you?"

Mrs. Whedon shrugged. She was wearing a track suit in avocado, which was her signature color. Except for the hospital gowns she'd been in, I'd never seen her in any other color.

"I'm all right. A little tired, even though I've been sleeping for weeks. That's why I wanted to talk to you all at once. Did Becky tell you what happened?"

"She...doesn't remember much," I said. "Other than the victim touched her."

Her face fell. "Victim. Why didn't you tell me?" She glanced up at the judge. "Darn. I didn't mean to kill him."

Everyone around us gasped.

Greg cleared his throat. "Maybe start at the beginning," he said.

"I was walking through the park on my way to see the judge. I guess we're dating exclusively now, his idea not mine. So, it's okay for people to know."

People had known for years.

"You're not even looking at another man," the judge grumbled. "And you didn't technically murder him."

What did that mean?

"Might as well have. Lizzie, I understand he was a friend of yours, but it didn't look like it that night. Becky screamed bloody murder. When I walked in, she was fighting for her life. He kept trying to grab her and she was kicking and screaming.

"That's how I found them. In hindsight, he was probably trying to calm her down, but I yelled. And I guess he reacted by shoving her away.

"She slipped and hit her head on one of the shelves in the freezer." Gran shivered. "The most blood-curdling sound, I thought he'd killed her. He turned toward me and his eyes were wild, like a crazy man's. I just reacted. I kicked him in the—well, the last place men like to get kicked. He bent over. And then I gave him an uppercut. I grabbed the heaviest thing I could find. A big old frying pan."

She frowned, her mouth a tight line. "I must have got him good in the you know whats, because he hit the floor with his knees. That's when I hit him with everything I had. It was a bone-crunching sound." She shivered again. "His head spun hard to the right and he tried to stand up. But there was so much blood, his hand slipped and he hit his head again on that steel table.

"He was flat out.

"I opened the freezer door to get Becky out, but I must have slipped on the blood. The last thing I remember is opening that door."

This time she shuddered. "I'm not usually so klutzy. And I'm sorry for your loss, Lizzie. I promise you, I didn't mean to kill him. I just needed to get sweet Becky out of that freezer. And I—it looked like he was hurting her."

Lizzie was sobbing softly, but nodded. "I understand. I do. Anyone would have thought the same thing. I think he thought he was scaring me. He liked to do that, and then Becky—that poor, poor girl. She probably panicked. I would have."

Gran reached out for Lizzie's hand. "Hon, the judge told me that he was your ex and a good friend. I just want you to know, there's no excuse for what happened. I wish—just know that I was trying to protect Becky. That's all."

Lizzie took Gran's hand. "I believe you. It was just a terrible set of circumstances. He was a good man. I want you to know that. More so that you understand he never would have hurt Becky. She had a situation where she was attacked—and she reacted as any of us would. If he was alive, I'd kick him in the nuts. It was a really dumb thing he did."

Lizzie let go of Gran's hand. "I need to tell Becky. I think she might still wonder if she killed him."

"That was my first stop," Gran said. "I left her crying with relief in her mom and dad's arms. I just feel so awful about the whole thing."

Even in the dark, it was evident Gran had grown paler.

"Son, if you're going to take me to the pokey, I have one favor to ask, even though I don't have the right to," she said to Greg.

"No one is going to the pokey," the judge said angrily and then stared at my brother.

"Gran, I'm a man who learns from my mistakes. Last time I took you to the station, I nearly lost my job. I won't say that there won't be some sort of hearing. I have a feeling his family will demand it, but for now, we should get you home and in bed," Greg said.

"Thank goodness. I really wanted to sleep in my own bed one last time."

I glanced at my brother and the judge worriedly.

The judge closed his eyes and sighed. "I'll have to recuse myself but it was self-defense. And there's not a judge in this county who would say otherwise. I'm happy to talk to the family and tell them exactly that."

"Please forgive me," she said to Lizzie.

"Oh, Mrs. Whedon, I do. I promise. I appreciate you telling us so soon, but we really should get you home to rest. Your brain and your body have been through a lot."

"You're a good one, Lizzie, and one heck of a baker. I actually dreamed about your blueberry scones more than once when I was out."

Lizzie laughed, and kissed Gran's forehead. "I will bring you some over tomorrow."

That my new friend could be so forgiving proved that I had good instincts. Not that I needed that sort of affirmation.

By the time Jake and I made it home with George and Julia Roberts, I was exhausted, and at the same time my brain was still going a thousand miles a minute. I sat down on the couch, and Jake did the same.

"Are you okay?"

"Yes, that was a lot to process."

"I agree. Leave it to Gran to make the whole thing so dramatic."

I smiled. "Right. She wakes up from a coma. Throws on a green track suit and orders the judge to take her to Becky's room. And then carry her up two flights of stairs."

"I think he might be sweet on her," he joked.

"You think?" I laughed. It felt good. For the first time in weeks, it felt like I could relax. I leaned against his shoulder.

"Do you think she might go to jail? I mean the judge is pretty powerful in these parts, but Mort was a successful businessman, and his family pulls some weight in these parts."

"True. But think about it. His brother already figured that Mort had scared Becky. He seemed to take it well at the party when we all thought Becky killed him."

"What I can't get over is how does she have that kind of

arm strength?" Jake said.

I laughed again. "I asked her the same thing. She said it must have been all the weaving yarn and carrying around potting soil. She does love to knit and her garden."

Jake's face tightened. His mouth went into a straight line and his eyebrows drew together.

That was his *I need to talk to you about something important* face.

What now? My brain wasn't ready for drama. Had I missed something about the case?

"Seeing the judge and Gran tonight—there's been something I've been trying to do since before your birthday. I was going to do it on your birthday, but we were worried about George. And then again under the fireworks tonight—but that was sidetracked."

My heart skipped a beat.

He reached in his pocket and pulled out a velvet box.

"You always say your favorite place is on this couch with me and George, and now Julia Roberts," Jake said.

"I'd get on one knee, but I'm still having trouble with my ankle."

"Jake. You—I—"

He held up a hand. "Don't say anything yet. Just listen. I want to get this out before we're interrupted again. I love you, Ainsley. Every stinking thing about you. Your beautiful heart and equally gorgeous face. You smell like strawberries, and you have a brain that is so incredible.

"I love George and Julia. I love that you will do anything for your friends. Maybe not the dangerous part of that, but I respect the lengths you'll go to for them. I know we said we'd wait for this, but I don't want to. Not anymore. Life is short and I want to marry you, Ainsley McGregor, and you'd better say yes."

"I should have never told you I liked your bossy side," I said, and then winked at him.

He smiled back, and my heart tugged in my chest. There was never going to be a man I loved more than Jake. He was everything.

After opening the box, which held the most beautiful diamond, he waited patiently.

"You didn't actually ask me the question." I laughed.

His eyes went wide. "Ainsley, will you marry me?"

I started laughing, and he did too.

Our friends busted through the back door of my kitchen carrying champagne and glasses.

Everyone I loved, with the exception of Gran, surrounded us.

George barked.

"So is that a yes?"

I smiled. "Well…"

The End

Want more? Check out Ainsley and George Clooney's last adventure in *A Case for the Candle Maker*!

Join Tule Publishing's newsletter for more great reads and weekly deals!

If you enjoyed *A Case for the Cookie Baker,*
you'll love the other books in....

The Ainsley McGregor series

Book 1: *A Case for the Winemaker*

Book 2: *A Case for the Yarn Maker*

Book 3: *A Case for the Toy Maker*

Book 4: *A Case for the Candle Maker*

Book 5: *A Case for the Cookie Baker*

Available now at your favorite online retailer!

About the Author

Bestselling and award-winning author Candace Havens has had more than thirty novels published. She is one of the nation's leading entertainment journalists and has interviewed countless celebrities from George Clooney to Chris Pratt. She does film reviews on Hawkeye in the Morning on 96.3 KSCS.

Visit her website at candacehavens.com

Thank you for reading

A Case for the Cookie Baker

If you enjoyed this book, you can find more from all our great authors at TulePublishing.com, or from your favorite online retailer.

Made in the USA
Las Vegas, NV
06 November 2025